KINCAID

A PARANORMAL CASEBOOK

FICTION BY WILLIAM F. NOLAN

KINCAID

A PARANORMAL CASEBOOK

**WILLIAM F
NOLAN**

 ROCKET RIDE BOOKS

Rocket Ride Books—Fiction that takes you there.
www.rocketridebooks.com
inquiries@rocketridebooks.com

ISBN-13: 978-0-9823322-2-1
ISBN-10: 0-9823322-2-X

1. Title
2. Paranormal—William F. Nolan
3. Suspense—Horror
4. Mystery

PRINTED IN THE UNITED STATES OF AMERICA

With paranormal best
to ANTHONY ROTOLO

CONTENTS

INTRODUCTION

I TAKE SPECIAL DELIGHT in creating series characters: Logan the Sandman (*LOGAN'S RUN*), Sam Space, my wacky, Mars-based detective (*SEVEN FOR SPACE*), Bart Challis, my ultra-tough L.A. Eye (*THE WHITE CAD CROSS-UP*), and as this collection demonstrates, paranormal investigator David Kincaid.

Although Kincaid made his printed debut in "Pirate's Moon," written in the spring of 1986, his roots extend back to the fall of 1972, when I drafted a teleplay for producer Dan Curtis featuring paranormal investigator David Norliss (*THE NORLISS TAPES*). Norliss was set to star in his own TV series, but the project was killed by a writer's strike. However, I liked writing about a protagonist who delves in the paranormal. Thus, fourteen years later, David Norliss morphed into David Kincaid.

Assembled for the first time in collected book format, here are his three bizarre cases. I hope you enjoy reading them as much as I enjoyed writing them.

I may write about him again.

Or I may not.

Up to Fate, my mood of the moment, and how much I need the money.

For now—here's Kincaid.

W.F.N.
VANCOUVER, WA
2011

ONE

PIRATE'S MOON

ALTHOUGH WE'D NEVER MET, Dwight Robert Lee and I shared the same beach. Separated by several miles of sand, but with the same blue-green Pacific waters washing over us both. Me, wind-surfing near the Santa Monica pier, trying to forget a rough day with my tax accountant, using the ocean as personal therapy—until it got too dark and cold to stay in the water. Him, a few miles farther up the coast, at Pirate's Cove, doing nothing in particular, loose-limbed, just rolling with the waves, letting them take him where they would. Neither of us was in any hurry to go anywhere.

By the time the moon came out, riding clear of a massed cloud bank, I was home, wrestling a bachelor's steak onto my backyard barbecue. Dwight Robert Lee was still at the beach. Stretched on the cool sand in the sudden wash of moonlight. He wasn't going home that night. Not in his condition.

For one thing, his head was missing.

Naturally, I read about the discovery of his body in the *L.A. Times* the next morning. But I didn't personally get involved with the case for another week. Not until the afternoon Mike Lucero decided that he needed my help.

Mike is a close friend, so I'd better tell you about him. He's a homicide detective working out of the Malibu Sheriff's Station. Built like a weight lifter. Big, slab-muscled, with a wide grin that buries his eyes in sun wrinkles. Miguel Francisco Lucero. Oldest of nine children. He grew up on one of those small mountain villages in northern New Mexico where they believe in witches and *mal ojo*, the evil eye (helps him put up with me!). After he left the University of New Mexico with a degree in psychology, he headed for California. Wanted to be a cop. And since there's always a need for bilingual officers in the L.A. County Sheriff's Department, Mike got signed up fast.

He lives in Woodland Hills, in the western San Fernando Valley, with his wife, Carla, and a loud pair of twin five-year-old daughters. He's a good man and a good cop.

I met Mike three years ago, when he attended one of my psychic seminars. As a cop, he figured it would help if he could develop his psychic ability. We all have it, to one degree or another. Some more, some less. Just a matter of self-development. I'm into the world of the paranormal; it's what I do for a living. I teach, write, investigate, conduct seminars, hold personal consultations—the works. I don't expect everybody to believe in all the stuff I deal with (I'm still mentally struggling with a lot of it myself), but I do ask people to keep an open mind about our incredible universe and what might or might not be in it. In outer and inner space—the space inside our being. You, me, and the cosmic universe. A big package.

Anyhow, after listening to some of my ideas, Mike figured I was a certified nut case and we didn't see each other again for a year. Until the body of a teenage girl was found in Topanga Canyon with her throat cut. No clues. No suspects.

Mike came to me, reluctantly, and asked if I could help him crack the case. Brought along a ring found on the body. "You're the psychic," he growled, "so tell me what happened."

I couldn't. My psychic powers are quite limited. I sent him to a woman named Brenner in Pasadena. She "read" the dead girl's ring, and her mental visions eventually led Mike to the killer. Doesn't always work that way, but this time it did. Lucero was impressed.

We talked. Had dinner together. By evening's end, he gave me that slit-eyed grin of his and said, "Damn if I don't think we're friends. What do you think?"

Over the next two years I helped Mike on half a dozen cases. Not all of them were solved, but I gave each one my best shot. Which is why I am an official Sheriff's Consultant—with a shiny badge to prove it.

So here was big Mike Lucero, on a foggy coastal afternoon in May, sprawled across my living-room couch, sipping from a can of Diet Pepsi, talking about the dead man found under a pirate's moon.

"This guy was one bad dude," Mike declared. "They called him Stomper. That's because he enjoyed putting the boot to people he mugged." Mike took a swig from his Pepsi. "Dwight Robert 'Stomper' Lee. A sadistic sicko. Believe me, he was no loss to society."

I was across the room in a chair by the fireplace. Wasn't fire weather; it's just my best chair. "How come you know his name when the corpse was stripped and his head was missing? How'd you make the ID?"

"Body tattoo. Skull and crossbones on the right side of his chest. Which told us he belonged to the Henchmen."

"That outlaw cycle gang?"

"Right. Every member of the Devil's Henchmen has to carry a chest tattoo."

"Even their...*women?*"

"You bet. Anyhow, we figured he'd have a record and ran his prints. Bingo. Computer told us all we wanted to know about him."

"Except who killed him."

"Yeah." Mike nodded. Not that I personally give a damn. Whoever did it rated a medal—but I happen to be a cop and he happens to be a murder victim. So you play the game."

Mike shrugged his heavy shoulders.

"Why come to me on this one?" I asked him.

"Because we're zip on it. Absolute dead end. And because it's weird." He gave me his slitted grin. "You know I always bring the weirdos to you, Dave."

"So what's so weird about finding a cycle freak with his head missing? Maybe he ripped off another Henchmen's chick and they stomped the Stomper. Or it could be the work of a rival gang who took his head for a souvenir."

"Whoever did it took more than his head," said Mike.

I raised an eyebrow. "More?"

"The scumbag's heart was missing. Cut right out of the body." Mike reached into his jacket and handed me an object sealed in clear plastic—a beaded feather, with a complex pattern of bright threads wound through it. We found this at the beach near Lee's corpse. You know something about Indians, so I brought it here."

I told Mike a lot about my childhood—about my early years in Arizona on the Hopi Reservation. My parents worked there for the U.S. Bureau of Indian Affairs. After they died—in a desert flash flood when I was six—I grew close to an old, half-blind Hopi medicine man who became a father figure to me. He gave me my first real taste of the spiritual world when he taught me the metaphysical Hopi view of life. Later at the University of Arizona, I expanded my knowledge by studying Indian lore from a wide variety of tribes.

So Mike was right. I know something about Indians. I carefully examined the feather, turning it slowly in the air.

"Well?" Mike growled impatiently. "What tribe is it from?"

"None," I said.

"Huh?"

"I mean it's not from any Indian tribe in North America."

"Where then?"

"You got me. I've never seen one like it. How do you know this is connected with Lee's murder?"

"I don't," Mike admitted. "It could have washed up on the beach the same way he did."

"Have you tried a psychic?"

"Sure, a couple. The two you put me onto—the Brenner woman and that bearded guy in Santa Monica, Dorfman."

"What did they tell you?"

"A lot of nothing is what they told me." He scowled, scrubbing a hand along his cheek. "Claimed they couldn't get any kind of clear reading on it."

"Then maybe the feather's *not* related to Lee's death," I said, handing it back. "Could have been tossed into the ocean by anybody."

"Yeah." Mike sighed. "Who the hell knows?"

He put his empty soda can on the coffee table and stood up. "Well, thanks anyhow."

"Going already?"

"Have to. Carla's got dinner in the microwave. I promised her I'd be home early."

"Tell her I said hi."

"Sure." When he reached the door he turned to level a hard look at me. "When you gonna get married again?"

"Whoa, pal! Give me some time. The divorce papers have barely cooled. Besides, I'd forgotten how nice a little solitude can—"

"Don't give me the 'contented bachelor' bit," growled Mike, cutting me off. "You need a woman. Living alone is no damn good."

And he was gone before I could think of a snappy reply to that one.

A month later, in June, Lucero contacted me again. I'd been out of state, conducting a mind-expansion seminar outdoors in Arizona, and I got back to find Mike's recorded growl on my answering machine. His message was brief and to the point: "Another murder. And another damn feather. Call me."

When I reached him by phone at the station he seemed edgy. "'Bout time you got back. Where the hell were you?"

"In the Arizona desert earning my living," I said tersely. "You know, I'm not paid to be on call to the Malibu Sheriff's Department."

His toned softened. "Okay, okay...I'm out of line. But this has been a crappy week."

I eased back on the couch, the receiver cradled against my shoulder. "So tell me about the second feather."

"I'd rather show it to you. Can you come down to the station?"

"I guess so."

"Then I'll be waiting." And he rang off.

The ocean sun was laying its usual late-afternoon strips of hammered gold over the surface of the Pacific when I turned off the Coast Highway and rolled my little red CRX Honda into the parking area at the Malibu station.

Mike looked sour and angry when I walked into his office. Obviously, the case was at a standstill. He nodded toward a battered leather chair facing his desk. I took it.

"How'd your outdoor seminar go?"

"Could have been better. It rained both days."

"Manage to expand any females?"

"Is that suppose to be funny?"

"Just friendly concern."

Mike settled behind his work-cluttered desk, a scarred oak relic that looked like a thrift-shop reject. In fact, Mike's office was something less than sumptuous. It smelled of mildewed files and stale cigar smoke. But he fought a lot of wars here and wasn't about to change anything.

I put out a hand. "Let me see it."

He gave me the second plastic-sealed feather. It was almost identical to the first. Bright with beads and intricately threaded.

"What about the body?" I asked.

"Same MO. Head missing. Heart cut out."

"Tattoo on his chest?"

"No. This guy was no scummy biker. He was a real celebrity. Athlete. Olympic runner. Had his picture on the cover of *People* last month. They called him the 'California Iron Man.'"

"Eddie Lansdale?"

"Yeah, him." Mike took a cigar from his desk and ran a match flame carefully around the tip. "He was easy to identify. Had a missing thumb on his right hand. Born that way." He let out a deep sigh. "The newspapers are gonna have a field day with this one."

"Where was he found?"

"Santa Monica Mountains. Couple of honeymooners were backpacking into the area when their mutt ran into this cave and began digging like crazy. Lansdale was buried there—*with* the feather. We still don't know what the hell it means."

His cigar had gone out and he was running a fresh flame over it.

"I'd like to take both feathers to someone I know. An anthropologist. He might be able to help." I looked at Mike. "What do you say?"

"I say they're the only clues we've got. I'm not suppose to let them out of my sight." He hesitated. "But go ahead, *take* the damn things. See what you can find out about 'em."

He opened his desk again and gave me the other feather.

"I'll be careful with your only clues," I said.

Mike grunted. He was still looking sour when I left his office. But at least he had his cigar going.

On-campus parking at UCLA is usually a hassle, but I got the CRX stashed neatly on a lot close to my target: Haines Hall. Home of Sidwick Sims Oliver, B.A., M.A., Ph.D. And the chairman of the Department of Anthropology.

Sid looked more like a Texas linebacker than a university professor, with his wide shoulders and bulky torso, but a pair of thick-lensed tortoiseshell glasses testified to his bookish character.

"Kincaid! Happy to see you!" He greeted me in his usual expansive manner with a crushing bear hug. (He never called me David.) Then he stepped back, frowning. "You trying out for Wild Bill Hickok?"

He referred to my fringed-buckskin shirt, silver Indian belt, and tooled-leather boots.

"I'm a desert critter, remember? Sun and sand and cacti. Haven't been in a suit since my Uncle Jack was buried. And that was three years ago."

Sid chuckled, a bass rumble. "To each his own!"

We were standing in the hall, flanked by shelves of native artifacts from a dozen world cultures. He waved me into his office. Which was as neat as he was. A place for everything and everything in its place. With all his papers in neat little piles. Freud would have called him anal retentive.

"I need your expertise," I told him as Sid handed me a minicarton of fresh carrot juice from his office fridge. He selected mango juice for himself. We sat down, facing one another.

"You helping the police on another case?"

I nodded. "Yeah. The Sheriff's Department. This one involves two headless corpses found in the Malibu area."

"*Two!*" Sid pursed his thick lips. "I read about the headless cycle gentlemen. But...*another!*"

"It'll be in the papers by tonight," I said. "With all the gory details. Well..." I corrected myself. "Not *all* the details. It won't mention these."

And I produced the two feathers.

He took the plastic-covered objects gingerly into his large hands, peering myopically. The sun from the window fired the beads to points of brightness.

I leaned toward him. "Can you identify them?"

"Of course I can," he said, raising his head to me. "They're from Papua New Guinea. The threading and the beads are ceremonial. Stone Age stuff."

I blinked at him. "What are feathers from the Stone Age doing next to dead bodies in Malibu?"

"I didn't say they were actually *from* the Stone Age," Oliver grumbled. "It is simply that tribal customs in New Guinea have remained constant since that era. As to their connection with your two corpses, that is up to you and your police friends to determine."

"Can you tell me what specific tribe these are from?"

"No. That would be extremely difficult for me to ascertain. I'm no expert on New Guinea. But I know someone who is."

"Here in the department?"

He shook his head. "A freelance professional journalist. Kelly Rourke's done research in the mountains of Papua. You could talk to Rourke."

"Sounds good."

Oliver flipped through the cards in his Rolodex, scribbled on a notepad, tore off the page, and handed it to me. "Rourke has an apartment in the American Comic Book Company building on Ventura. That's Studio City."

I scanned the note pad. "Phone?"

"No, Rourke hates phones. Just go on over. Say I sent you. Odds are you'll get your information."

"Sid…" I clapped him on the shoulder. "I owe you a lunch."

"Solve the case and we'll celebrate. You can buy me champagne."

"For *lunch*?"

"Brunch. A champagne brunch."

And I had to submit to another crushing bear hug before I got out of there.

I took Sunset from UCLA, passing all the giant showbiz billboards along the Strip, gaudily promoting rock groups with names like Shiva, Orange Love, and The Little Big Men, then turned left on Laurel Canyon and made my way up and over the twisting snake of road that divides Hollywood from the San Fernando Valley. The little CRX danced through the curves like a prima ballerina and I got to Ventura Boulevard in jig time.

The American Comic Book Company was on the second floor. I climbed the carpeted steps, with a jagged red lightning bolt painted on the wall, to a wide landing with two doors facing one another. The first was open, and I peered into a comic fiend's paradise. Wall-to-wall superheroes in multicolored underwear.

The second door was closed. On pebbled glass, lettered in black, were the bold words: GO AWAY. I DON'T LIKE STRANGERS. AND IF YOU'RE SELLING ANYTHING—DIE!

I hoped Sid was right about my getting cooperation. Mr. Rourke didn't seem the friendly type.

I rapped on the glass. A red-haired knockout in a tight black turtleneck and thigh-hugging plum stretch pants opened the door and glared at me. "Can't you *read*?"

"Must have the wrong office," I said. "I'm looking for Mr. Rourke. He's a writer."

"You're looking at him," she said. "Only I'm a *her*."

"You certainly are," I said.

She smiled at my lewd enthusiasm. "My mother's maiden name was Kelly. She planned on giving it to her son, but I came along instead. I'm always surprising people."

"You sure surprised me," I admitted. "I'm David Kincaid. Sid Oliver sent me here. He said that I should talk to you."

"About what?"

"A double murder that may extend back to the Stone Age."

That one got me inside.

"...and when I needed more data, Sid suggested you. So here I am."

"Let's see the feathers," she said.

I gave them to her. Their glowing colors contrasted with the dimness of the room. Kelly told me she kept the curtains drawn because she could think better that way; raw sunlight bothered her when she was writing. Well, as Sid would say, to each his own.

Her place was neat and comfortable. Big-pillowed sofas (we were sitting on one), antique chairs, oil paintings of ocean sunsets, and a cabinet of painted plates behind glass. Plus books. Lots of books. Writers have books like alley cats have fleas. Comes with the territory.

After she'd examined the feathers, Kelly walked to a shelf, selected one of the books, brought it over to me. The title was in red: *Tribal Customs of Papua New Guinea.* By Nigel somebody.

"New Guinea's part of Australia, isn't it?" I asked.

"Used to be, but they got their independence in 1975." She flipped the book open. "Look at these."

The photos were in full color, showing gaudily painted natives with bones through their noses jumping up and down inside a big bamboo hut of some kind. And they all wore feathers.

"That's a Purari ceremonial dance," said Kelly. "The masked dancers in red and black represent ghosts of the dead, and that tall character, the really ugly one in the middle, he's a witch doctor. Chases away evil spirits. Check the feathers he's wearing."

She placed one of Mike's murder clues next to a close-up photo in the book. "Notice the pattern—the way the beads are threaded into the main body of the feather."

"Yeah...they're the same."

"And your missing heads and hearts tie right in."

"To what?"

"To their tribal customs." She gave me a steady look. "The Purari were cannibals."

I let out a long breath as Kelly continued.

"They severed the heads for luck. Or what *we'd* call luck. Sleeping on a skull at night was considered strong magic."

"And the hearts?"

"They devoured them. In order to absorb the victim's *mana*, or life force. Eating the heart was supposed to give them the victim's strength."

I leaned back into the pillow, turning one of the feathers slowly in my right hand.

"Could these be fake? I mean, not the real McCoy?"

"Nope," Kelly said flatly. "For one thing, the thread pattern is far too subtle and complex."

"Meaning what?"

"Meaning that only a real Papua New Guinean would know how to make these. Most likely a tribal witch doctor."

"We don't have cannibal witch doctors in L.A.," I said.

"They don't have them in New Guinea, either. Not anymore. Cannibalism has been extinct there for a long time."

"Then how do you explain all this?"

"I don't. But I think we should go talk to the Australian consul general."

"We?"

"As a writer, I want to follow through on this. Might get a piece for *The New Yorker* out of it. Okay with you?"

"I never say no to a beautiful woman."

Kelly smiled sweetly. "Bull," she said.

The abstract stained-glass tower of St. Basil's Cathedral speared its long shadow across Wilshire Boulevard, darkening the marbled entrance court of Paramount Plaza. Kelly and I walked through the tall doors of an elegant twenty-story stone-and-black-glass office building and took the elevator to the seventeenth floor.

Above an impressive continental shield, featuring an embossed kangaroo, the words AUSTRALIAN CONSULATE GENERAL were gold-leafed on the door of Suite 1742.

We went in. Several pale orange couch chairs faced a wall of shelved reference books. A framed painting of Queen Elizabeth II, in royal regalia, was on the wall next to a large contour map of Australia.

Kelly walked over to a stiff-faced lady in a glass-fronted reception booth and told her we were here to see the man himself, Sir Leslie Fraser-Shaw.

"Do you have an appointment with Sir Leslie?"

"I called in," I told her. "He knows me. He's agreed to see us."

The stiff-faced receptionist verified this on her intercom, then ushered us into the sanctorum.

As we entered, Fraser-Shaw rose like a white-suited Buddha from a desk the size of a polished iceberg. He was a wide-bodied man in his sixties, with a florid complexion and deeply pouched eyes. He gave us a political smile.

"Ah, Kelly, my dear...safely back from the untrammeled wilds of Mongolia, I see."

"Yep, two weeks ago," she said.

"Splendid!" Fraser-Shaw swung his puffy eyes in my direction. "And you are...?"

"David Kincaid. From the untrammeled wilds of Malibu."

"Ah, yes." His smile wavered. He led us to a long white sofa. "Please make yourselves comfortable."

Sir Leslie settled down next to us, folding his small pink hands across the bulk of his stomach.

"Now, my dear," he said to Kelly, "just how may I be of service to you? Planning another Australian trip?"

"No, not this time," she said. "Mr. Kincaid is assisting the police on a homicide. Two of them, in fact. The murders may involve tribal Papua."

"How very peculiar," said Fraser-Shaw.

"Our purpose in coming here," I said, "is to find out what you can tell us about people from Papua New Guinea who may now be living in the Los Angeles area."

"This is the *Australian* Consulate," Sir Leslie said firmly. "We have no legal ties to Papua New Guinea."

"I realize that—but since there is no New Guinea consulate..."

Fraser-Shaw shifted in his chair, tenting his delicate pink fingers. "Of course there are many Australians here in Southern California, but I really don't believe there are any residents from Papua New Guinea. At least, not to my knowledge."

"There was a ceremonial feather left at the site of each murder," I said. "From Papua."

"They're definitely authentic tribal feathers," Kelly declared. "Very much the real thing."

"Your murderer could be a collector," said Fraser-Shaw. "He could have purchased the feathers in Papua—leaving them as, one might say, his personal calling cards."

"That's possible," I admitted.

Sir Leslie checked his watch and stood up, letting us know

the meeting had ended.

"I do wish I could spend more time discussing this matter with you," he said, "but I am victim to a crowded schedule."

"Appreciate your seeing us, Sir Leslie," said Kelly, smiling at him.

He put a fleshy paw on her shoulder. "You are most welcome, my dear. And if I can be of any further help, do not hesitate to call on me."

"We just might," I said.

He nodded toward me. "Good luck with your enquiries, Mr. Kincaid."

I said thanks to that.

After a late dinner, I dropped Kelly off at her comic-book address, promising to "keep her in the picture" as the case progressed—*if* it progressed. Then I phoned Mike Lucero and filled him in on the Papua New Guinea angle. He was, to say the least, highly skeptical about the possibility of Stone Age cannibals in Los Angeles.

"But it explains the feathers," I told him.

"Sure it does," he said. "Now all we have to do is find a *real* explanation. Just bring 'em back to me in the morning, okay?"

"In the morning," I said.

I drove home under a full moon, turning off Malibu Canyon Road at Las Virgenes and aiming the CRX up the mile-long climb past the Hindu Temple to road's end near the Cottontail Ranch. I eased the Honda down the curving gravel drive fronting my place, got out, and took a deep breath—inhaling the sweet scent of pine, sage, and oleander. And even this far inland, a sea wind brought me the faint iodine smell of the Pacific. There are worse places to live, and I was smiling as I keyed open the front door.

Inside, I experienced a neck-prickling sensation that told me I wasn't alone.

I spun from the door as three tall, heavily muscled figures came for me, brandishing wicked-looking knives and spears. They had bones in their noses. The moonlight played across naked chests and painted faces, and all I could think of was how surprised Mike Lucero would be to see his ole buddy being attacked at home by three frothing Stone Age cannibals.

I dropped into a defensive crouch as a bamboo spear whistled past my left ear to bury itself in the wall. I figured it was time to make all those painful hours of karate practice pay off.

I took out the first guy with a *yoko-geri*—a powerful side kick to the neck with the outside edge of my right boot. He went down like chopped timber.

I pivoted toward the second guy, into a *mawashi-zuki*, thrusting my left fist forward into a roundhouse half-circle from the hip to the side of his head. He crashed backward, taking a lamp table down with him.

The third guy was the biggest, with a long, raised scar puckering his right cheek, and he was charging in with a raised blade big enough to impress Jim Bowie. I ducked under the glittering arc of his knife and put the elbow of my right arm hard into his ribs—the always effective *empi-uchi.* One of his bones cracked, like a dry twig breaking. He grunted and dropped the knife, staggering, his eyes wild, lips pulled back from the pain.

I was gearing up for more action when the three of them decided they didn't like my magic. The knife-wielder scooped up his blade and the spear-thrower retrieved his spear. Then, like three night shadows, they left the way they'd come in, sliding through the living-room window and instantly vanishing into the thick brush and trees.

When Mike Lucero answered the phone his opening words were fogged with sleep. "Yeah...who...who's calling?"

"Kincaid."

"*Dave?*... It's damn late! Don't you ever go to bed?"

"Being attacked by cannibals tends to keep me awake."

He was really pissed now. "You call me in the middle of the friggin' night because you're having a friggin' dream about cannibals?"

"No dream, Mike. These three boys were the genuine article. Feathers, body paint, bones in the nose—like they stepped right out of a Stone Age time machine."

"I thought you didn't do drugs," Mike growled.

Now *I* was pissed and allowed the anger to edge my voice. "I don't, and you know it. I'm telling you straight—when I got home tonight three painted savages with knives and spears were waiting for me. They damn well tried to *kill* me. Without my karate training I would have bought the farm."

"Okay, okay...I'll take your word about the attack. But whoever they were, they weren't Stone Age savages."

"Who were they then?"

"Could've been three of the Henchmen, playing native. To go with the feathers they planted on the two bodies. Trying to freak you off the case."

"You think the Henchmen are responsible for both murders?"

"I'm not ruling out the idea. I questioned as many of those slimeballs as I could round up—and they're a mean bunch of mothers, lemme tellya. They could be using all this New Guinea savage crap as a smoke-screen."

"But *why*? What's the point of it all? If they wanted to snuff the Stomper and the Olympic guy for some reason, why not just kill them outright, with no frills? Why the big masquerade?"

"Could be their sick sense of humor. These people are *twisted*, Dave."

"I don't buy it," I said firmly. "It's just too bizarre."

"Look." Mike sighed. "Let's talk at the station. I gotta get back to sleep or I won't be worth a damn tomorrow. I'm just glad you're okay." He hesitated. "You *are* okay, right?"

"I'm fine. Not a scratch."

"Then can we talk about this in the morning? You can file a full report."

"Sure. In the morning."

And I rang off.

When I woke up at ten, the sun was hiding out. A fog had blown in from the ocean, making everything gray and cobwebby. Which was how I felt. I showered, dressed. And fixed myself Swedish pancakes for breakfast. Whenever I get depressed I treat myself to Swedish pancakes. Stomach therapy.

I was in no hurry to talk to Mike Lucero. We'd said all there was to say at this point, and I figured I'd rather look into Kelly's deep green eyes than Mike's scowling cop's mug. So I phoned her.

She seemed delighted to hear from me. "I was going to call *you*," she said. "I want to take you someplace special today. To see a bloke I know."

"A *bloke*? That's Aussie talk."

"It's the only clue I'll give you," she said. And she laughed.

Forty-five minutes later I picked her up in front of her comic-book building in Studio City and asked where we were headed.

"For Yuppie Heaven," she said. And her green eyes glinted.

I knew where that was: the oh-so-hip area of neoned "in" shops and cafés stretching for several blocks along Melrose, below Hollywood. With names like the Last Wound-up, Indiana Joan's, and the Big Bravo. Where all the young, upwardly mobile couples twitter over the latest craze in clothes, videos, records, collectibles, and books.

On the way over I told Kelly about my violent brush with the Stone Age. She was shocked when she realized I wasn't kidding.

"Mike figures they were cycle freaks, coming on as natives," I said.

"He's wrong," Kelly declared. "From your description, I'd say they were real."

"Real *savages*?"

"Not in the sense one associates with the term. But definitely people from Papua New Guinea."

"But Fraser-Shaw told us there aren't any people from New Guinea in L.A."

"He said he didn't *know* of any. Well, I do."

"Yesterday you didn't."

"That was then and this is now. I did some phoning. That's why we're going where we're going. You'll see."

"Okay, but I am running out of patience. Where the hell *are* we going?"

"The Down-Under," said Kelly.

The place is owned by a female pop singer from Australia. When you go inside there are dozens of framed pictures of her along the walls. And near the back there's this big screen with constantly running footage of her performing but with no soundtrack. It's kind of spooky, watching her sing with no words coming out.

"It wouldn't be appropriate to our overall atmosphere."

That's what the manager of Down-Under told me when I asked him why we couldn't hear the singer singing. He was the Aussie "bloke" Kelly had taken me to meet. Derek Newcombe, a tall string bean of a guy. Seems his parents used to work with the natives in Papua New Guinea before the big split with Australia.

He was standing behind the planed-wood "Aussie Milk Bar" (in red neon letters) as Kelly and I perched on two high stools at the counter.

"What'll it be, mates?" Derek asked.

"Vegemite, and a Blue Heaven milk shake," said Kelly.

"I'll just go with the Blue Heaven," I said. And turned to her. "What's Vegemite?"

"It's great! Everybody in Australia has it for breakfast. Highly nutritious, too."

When her order arrived, with the Vegemite spread darkly over buttered wheat, it looked exactly like cinnamon toast. And I *love* cinnamon toast.

"Want a bite?" she asked.

"You bet," I said.

"Chew it thoroughly," advised Derek.

I bit into Vegemite-covered toast and began chewing. *"Gah!"* I sputtered, barely able to swallow the stuff.

"I don't think he cares for it," Derek said to Kelly.

She nodded. "It's an acquired taste." And she dug into her order with sickening enthusiasm.

"What the hell's it *made* of?"

"Yeast, mainly."

"Yech! No wonder."

Two big stuffed kangaroos flanked the bar, and I would rather have bitten into one of them.

Then Kelly got to the point of our visit.

"Derek, on the phone this morning, you told me that you know for a fact that there are at least two to three dozen people from Papua New Guinea living in Los Angeles area. We've come here to find out about them."

Newcombe compressed his lips and scratched his head, looking like Stan Laurel. And he also had Laurel's sad eyes. "Well...maybe I spoke out of turn."

"What's that suppose to mean?" I asked him.

"These people...they're very private. Keep to themselves. They don't like to mix with outsiders."

I nodded. "With anyone who isn't from Papua New Guinea, you mean?"

"Right, mate. Exactly right." He even had Laurel's high, piping voice—but with a thick Aussie accent. "I wouldn't advise attempting to make contact with any of them, if that's what you had in mind."

"Really?" I said. "Well, three of 'em sure tried to make contact with *me* last night."

"I don't follow you, mate," said Derek.

"Forget it," I said. "Just tell us where we can find these people."

"I'm not sure...if I should..." Newcombe looked uncertain.

"C'mon, Derek, what's the problem?" Kelly demanded. "We just need to ask them a few questions. It's no big deal."

"All right then, luv," said Newcombe. "Go down to Third and San Pedro. There's a bar on the corner—the Imunu. That's where they congregate. Kind of a meeting place for them."

"How do we know when they'll be there?" I asked.

"Or what they look like?"

"My father goes there to drink with them sometimes," said Newcombe. "He told me that this tall bloke from Papua named Dibela works there days as a bartender. He might answer whatever questions you have. But I wouldn't count on it."

"How do we recognize Dibela?" asked Kelly.

"That's easy. Bloke has a right fierce scar along his right cheek."

I did a double take on that one. Jackpot! The spearthrower!

It was time to move.

"Thanks, mate," I said, steering Kelly toward the door. She was still nibbling Vegemite on the way out.

I phoned Mike Lucero and told him to meet me at the Imunu in an hour and that I'd explain why when he got there. Then we took the Hollywood Freeway into central L.A. I parked the CRX in a lot a half-block east of the bar. The afternoon sun was gradually sliding down the edge of the western sky, lengthening our shadows as we moved along San Pedro.

Walking through this seedy, down-at-the-heels area, passing the battered, grimed storefronts, decorated by dopers, winos, grifters, pimps, and prostitutes, was a depressing business. This was another, darker world, full of poverty and violence and smashed lives. Derek had it right; we didn't belong here.

The Imunu was a typical product of the area. A soot-blackened COORS sign flickered in dying neon behind a grease-filmed window. The bar's name had been painted on a strip of peeling wood above the front door, but the last two letters had flaked away, leaving only IMU on the weathered board.

Inside, the air reeked of sour tobacco and spilled beer. "This place would give Count Dracula the creeps," I muttered to Kelly.

It wasn't crowded. Perhaps a dozen drinkers huddled over their glasses at tables and booths, regarding us with suspicious eyes as we crossed the smoke-dimmed room to the bar.

"Shouldn't we wait for your cop friend?" Kelly asked me. I'd told her about the scar. "This Dibela guy might go for you again."

"Not in public," I said. "And not without his pals. I just want to make sure he's the same bird before Mike gets here to put the cuffs on him."

"Okay." Kelly shrugged. "We'll play it your way."

The guy behind the bar was tall and black and mean-looking, but he *didn't* have a scar on his cheek.

"What you want?" he demanded, with a glare.

"Does a man named Dibela work here?" I asked.

"Maybe."

I slid a ten-dollar bill across the counter. He closed his hand over it like a shark's jaw, not looking at the money. He kept glaring at me.

I waited. "Well?"

"He took off early today—couple of minutes before you came in. Said he had something special he had to do. Might still be able to catch him." The bartender flicked his head toward the rear of the building in a quick gesture. "Got an old Ford pickup truck. Keeps it round back. If it's there, he's there."

"Thanks," I said, and hustled outside with Kelly. We sprinted for the lot behind the building. Dibela was just getting into the pickup. We got a side flash of his scarred face as he climbed into the truck.

"Is that the guy?" asked Kelly.

"Yep. Only his spear is missing." I looked around, the muscles in my jaw tightening. "Where the hell's Lucero? Guy's gonna be long gone in another two seconds!"

Then Mike's unmarked car rolled up to us. Talk about the nick of time! He waved from the window. "Saw you hop around the building. What's going down?"

I climbed into Mike's car, pulling Kelly in after me. I'd introduce them later. "See that guy in the Ford?"

It passed us, pulling onto San Pedro.

"Yeah, so what?"

"So follow him—but don't let him know he's picked up a tail. He's one of the three weirdos who attacked me. I figure he could lead us to the others."

"You've been a busy little bee since last night," Mike declared, moving out into the traffic flow.

"You packing your .38?" I asked.

He patted his coat. "Always."

"Good. We just might need it."

Dibela had no idea he was being tailed, but Mike was careful anyhow, staying far enough back to keep out of his driving mirror. Our boy cleared downtown L.A. and got onto the Ventura Freeway, with us right behind him.

As we drove I told Mike all about Kelly and Derek Newcombe and filled in the details of the night attack.

"And you're a hundred percent sure the guy we're after was one of them?" he asked.

"Hundred percent," I said. And told them about the scar.

He nodded, smiling faintly. It was the kind of smile I'd seen on his face before, when a tough case was coming into focus. "Sounds like you two are really on to something."

Kelly leaned toward him. "Then you're ready to believe us now—about the New Guinea tie-in to the murders?"

"I'd be a fool not to, at this point," he said. "Wacko as it seems, you've got me convinced we're chasing a freakin' cannibal down the Ventura Freeway!"

And we all grinned.

Dibela took the off ramp for Malibu Canyon Road, heading toward the coast. He didn't give any indication he'd seen us as Mike made the same turn, three cars behind the pickup.

The road twisted through rolling hills the color of lion pelts, with the lowering sun tinting the distant horizon.

"When you didn't show up at the station this morning, I began feeling guilty," Mike said.

I looked at him. "Why guilty?"

"The way I put you off last night, right after you'd practically been killed. As if my getting some extra shut-eye was more important than what you had to tell me."

"Hey, Mike, there was nothing you could have done. I just wanted you to know what happened."

"I still feel guilty about it. Then today, when you didn't show or call in, I began to worry—that maybe those three creeps had come back for you. So I drove over to your place to check it out. When you didn't answer, I forced a window to get inside, but you were gone."

"I meant to call you earlier, but Kelly took me under her wing."

"I have very soft feathers," she said.

Mike chuckled deep in his throat. "Seems you two make a good team. And if I do say so, a damn handsome couple."

I could see where this was heading, with Mike Cupid trying to set up a new soulmate for his ole buddy Dave. Another ten miles and he'd have us married.

The road now sliced between Malibu Canyon's sheer walls, with steeply rising sun-shadowed cliffs of tumbled granite on our left. California can look like many states, and right now it looked like the canyon country of Arizona. Hard to believe, at this moment, that a big blue ocean was waiting just over the ridge.

There was only one car between us and the Ford pickup when Dibela swung abruptly off the highway onto a narrow dirt trail leading into the mountains.

The sudden route change took Mike by surprise, and we skidded over some rough ground before reversing to complete the turn. By then the Ford was out of sight around a twist in the trail.

"This is no road," Mike grumbled. "Where the hell's he *going*?" He lifted his head, eyes slitted against the sky. "Nothin' up there but trees and rock. It's all raw wilderness."

"You found the second body in the mountains," I reminded him. "Maybe these New Guinea boys have some kind of headquarters up here."

"Makes sense," said Kelly. "This terrain is a lot like the mountains of Papua. Probably makes them feel right at home."

The dirt trail looped and bumped us upward, full of deep cuts and half-buried stones. Fit for coyotes, not cars. We were following the Ford's dust cloud, so there was no way Dibela could spot us behind him.

When the dust thinned, Mike slowed to a crawl, knowing Dibela had stopped somewhere just ahead. He drove off the trail into heavy chaparral, shielding the car.

"We walk from here," Mike said. "Stay right behind me, and keep to the trees. We don't want to be seen." He slipped the .38 from its clamshell holster, checked the load. "No telling what we'll run into."

With Mike leading, we proceeded cautiously through the trees paralleling the dirt trail. The sun had now dropped below the horizon, and an early-evening chill, blown in from the ocean, was settling over the mountains. We were moving through scented stands of eucalyptus, oak, and sycamore. There were king snakes and rattlers in these mountains, and I hoped we wouldn't be stepping on any. Or on a mountain lion's tail.

"You okay?" I asked Kelly.

"Sure." She nodded. Her hair was like polished brass in the sunless twilight. "Just glad I am not wearing high heels."

We were into a screening mass of tangled chamisa when Mike raised a warning hand. "Keep your heads down. We're coming up on something."

We arrived at the edge of a large clearing—and from our hiding place in the brush we saw Dibela's rusted-out truck parked behind a long, roughly constructed board shack.

"He's probably inside," said Mike, keeping his voice low. If there were any guards around, we didn't want to attract their attention.

At the farther side of the clearing was a second structure,

much larger than the shack, raised from the ground on a platform of thick wooden stilts and made of what I guessed was thatched bamboo.

"Do you recognize that?" I asked Kelly. "Looks native to me."

"It is," she said softly. "A tribal ceremonial house...called a House of Skulls."

"Sounds cozy," I said. "Just the place for a family picnic."

"What kind of ceremonies go on in a joint like that?" asked Mike.

"Different kinds," Kelly replied, "but they all center around tribal magic."

"Something's sure going on in there right now," I said, as a rhythmic pulsing of drums began, backed by chanting voices. That's when we saw the door of the shack open and our boy Dibela emerge. Dressed just the way he was when he attacked me—a loin-cloth around his waist and his dark-bronze flesh daubed with colored paints. He had a bone through his nose, with a mass of feathers decorating his head. And he carried a spear.

Mike shot me an incredulous look.

"Dibela is more than a bartender," said Kelly. "He's also a tribal witch doctor."

We watched him cross the clearing and enter the House of Skulls. The chanting inside changed pitch, becoming more intense, almost frenzied.

Mike swung his head toward Kelly. "What would you guess they're up to?"

"Impossible to say from here."

"Then it looks like we go have ourselves a gander," Mike declared.

We scanned the area for guards. It looked safe. Guess they felt secure up here in he middle of nowhere. With Mike lead-ing, we sprinted across the clearing, ducked between stilts, and crouched in the dry mustard grass beneath the House of Skulls.

Directly above, the platform juddered under pounding feet—and the sound of the drums and chanting voices washed around us, a sea of alien sounds.

We crawled to a better vantage point. Through a wide opening in the platform we could see more than two dozen natives, wearing wigs of fiber and bark, and necklaces of teeth, their dark bodies decorated with shells and colored seeds.

Many of the dancers carried bamboo spears and bone daggers, their skin painted in bizarre patterns, feathers waving as they swayed to the throbbing drums.

The interior walls were crowded with painted wooden shields and grotesquely carved tribal masks—and, of course, with skulls. Lots of skulls, with gaping, eyeless sockets and hanging jaws of yellowed bone. I figured a couple of them had been lopped off the bodies of Stomper Lee and Eddie Lansdale. God knew where the others came from.

Then I heard Mike draw in his breath sharply. "They've got a guy tied up in there!" he whispered.

He was right. At the far end of the platform, on a makeshift altar, we could see their latest victim, a young man stripped to the waist with his hands and feet securely bound. His neck rested on a crude wooden block, and it was obvious they intended to behead him. *And* cut his heart out.

That's what this damn ceremony was all about. This was the "something special" Dibela left work early for. Another ritual murder.

"Here, take this," Mike said, handing his .38 to me. "I'm going to the car and call for some backup. We gotta stop this before it's too late."

"I'm no good with a gun," I protested. "You might need it if you run into trouble."

"I'll be okay," Mike declared. "If they begin the main action before I get back—the head and heart bit—then start shooting. They can't stand up against bullets with the weapons they have."

"And what happens when I run out of bullets?"

"Cops'll be here by then."

And he ducked away from us, running low across the clearing in the direction of the car.

Lucero didn't get far. Two big natives who were rounding the shack spotted him, and loosed their spears. One missed; the other didn't.

Mike was down with a bamboo spear through his right shoulder.

"Bastards!" I muttered, and brought up the gun. I was ready to fire when Kelly grabbed my arm.

"Don't!" she warned. "Save your bullets until they're really needed. If we reveal ourselves now, *nobody* has a chance."

"Okay...I guess that makes sense." I lowered the .38, sweating. The palms of my hands were slick and my jaw muscles ached. This case was no longer colorful; it had turned deadly and frightening. I was shaking with tension.

The two natives dragged Lucero to his feet, and one of them jerked the spear loose. Mike let out a cry of agony. The spear point had gone through the soft flesh of his upper shoulder, and there was a lot of blood coming from the wound. Plus a lot of pain. But he was not seriously hurt.

Not yet.

Kelly and I ducked back into the shadows beneath the platform as the two natives passed us, forcing Mike ahead of them into the House of Skulls.

Inside, a wave of hostile cries was directed at Mike. Dibela danced around him, shaking his spear, teeth bared like a hungry wolf.

Then another native emerged from the clearing. He hurried into the House of Skulls, spoke intently to Dibela. The witch doctor left for the shack, remained inside for a few moments, then returned to the ceremony.

"Something's going on at the shack," I said.

"What should we do?" Kelly faced me, her green eyes shaded with concern. "Should one of us try for the car?"

"No," I told her. "They'll be posting new guards now that Mike's been spotted. We have to stay right here."

Sure enough, just as I finished speaking, three painted natives, armed with spears, left the ceremonial house and began prowling around the clearing.

"I'm sure they won't think of looking under here," whispered Kelly. "We'll be safe for a while."

"Yeah," I muttered, gripping the .38 tightly in my right fist. "For a while."

"They're putting Mike on the altar with that other guy," Kelly pointed out. "That means—"

"I *know* what it means."

We watched and listened in shock as the drums began a faster beat; the dancing intensified, and the chanting mounted in volume. Things were heating up.

Dibela approached the altar. He'd replaced his spear with what was obviously a ceremonial blade. He waved it in the air, and the frenzied dancers let out a howl.

"He's gonna *do* it!" I told Kelly. "He's gonna lop off Mike's head!"

"Then I guess...it's time for you to start shooting," said Kelly.

My hand was shaking as I brought up the gun, aiming at Dibela through the gap in the flooring.

I had the .38 in both hands, trying to steady my aim, when that bronzed devil raised the blade full above him, ready to bring it down on Mike's neck. His eyes gleamed and a smile puckered his scarred face. The chanting was really crazed.

"Dave!" Mike yelled. "Shoot the sonuvabitch before he *kills* me!"

My finger was about to squeeze the trigger when three loud shots, like popping firecrackers, stunned the dancers into silence.

Dibela slowly turned from the altar, blood gouting from his head and chest. His glazed eyes were already dead as he dropped the blade and sprawled forward across the floor.

"It's Fraser-Shaw!" I gasped.

The rotund, white-suited consul general was standing in the doorway of the House of Skulls, a thin spiral of blue-gray smoke curling from the barrel of the big .45 automatic in his right hand.

Kelly and I lost no time in making our presence known. We scrambled from our hiding place and ran into the ceremonial house like two happy kids.

Fraser-Shaw had introduced himself and was cutting Mike and the other victim loose, with both of them babbling their thanks, when we arrived on the scene. The natives, utterly silent, had drawn back against the walls. I swung the .38 toward them, but they didn't seem to offer any threat. Their sick little show was over.

"Ah," said Fraser-Shaw, turning to face us. "Miss Rourke and Mr. Kincaid. I had no idea you were here."

"That goes double for us," I said. "Where did you come from? And how did you find this place? Are you alone?"

"Please." He raised a hand. "One question at a time, Mr. Kincaid. First, we must inquire as to the condition of these two gentlemen."

"I'm okay," said Mike. "Not much feeling in my right arm, but a lot of the bleeding's stopped."

Kelly was using her neck scarf as a makeshift bandage. I handed the .38 back to Lucero, glad to be rid of the damn thing.

"And what about you, young man?" Fraser-Shaw asked.

"I'm still...kinda...shook-up," he answered.

"That's quite understandable," said Fraser-Shaw. "However, let me assure you that there is nothing more to fear. Now that I have killed their witch doctor, these people are rendered powerless. Their magic has been lost."

"Who are you?" Kelly asked the young man.

"McCammon," he said. "Ben McCammon. I'm assistant track coach at USC. These freaks kidnapped me from the athletic field last night. Man..." And he shook Fraser-Shaw's hand vigorously. "I'm just glad you showed when you did!"

"I'm going to call for backup," said Mike. "The rest of you stay here and keep an eye on these characters."

And Mike took off at a fast trot for the car.

Huddled close to the walls, the natives watched us silently.

Fraser-Shaw faced me. "Now, Mr. Kincaid, let me answer your questions. Your visit to my office yesterday roused my personal curiosity about the possible existence of a New Guinea cult in this area. I began an investigation and discovered that such a cult did indeed exist. The two recent murders were obviously the result of a brutal reversion to ancient tribal customs. Using my official status as a representative of Australia, I was able to locate one of these cultists. I found out he was going to attend some sort of ceremony."

"*This* ceremony?" I asked.

"Precisely," said the consul general. "I had no idea of its nature when I followed him here earlier today. Had I guessed it was another blood ritual, I would have brought along the authorities. I was, please understand, still operating from theory. However, shortly after I arrived here, I was discovered. I was taken prisoner and tied up in the shack. Eventually I managed to free myself. I recovered the weapon I'd brought here with me, and was fortunate enough to intervene before more blood was spilled." He smiled at me. "It's as simple as that."

I stared at him. "You're a remarkable man, Sir Leslie. Really remarkable."

"Why, thank you."

"That's not a compliment," I told him—spinning abruptly on my left heel and karate-kicking the .45 from his hand. I scooped up the automatic and leveled it at his fat gut.

Kelly and McCammon were starring at me as if I'd gone round the bend.

"Dave!" Kelly protested. "What's *wrong* with you? He saved our lives!"

"He was just trying to save his own. Trying to keep himself out of jail—but he didn't quite make it. Did you, mate?"

Fraser-Shaw glared at me, eyes frosted, lips compressed. "When the police arrive, I'll have you arrested for assault," he said tightly.

"Sure you will," I said. And smiled.

Of course, there was no assault charge. Sir Leslie Fraser-Shaw was the one they arrested. For murder. When the shack was searched, no binding ropes or tape or handcuffs were found—but the sheriff's deputies *did* find the carved wood spirit mask and body robe worn by Sir Leslie when he participated in the blood ceremonies.

He'd come here to share McCammon's death, and was in the act of preparing himself for the ceremony when Mike's capture abruptly changed his plans. That's when he called Dibela to the shack and instructed him to proceed with the ceremony. Now that the cult's latest victim was a homicide cop, Fraser-Shaw realized things had gone too far. It was time to bail out. Dibela had been the only one who could identify the consul general; the others had seen him *only* in his masked role as a spirit of the dead. Therefore, with the death of the witch doctor, any evidence connecting Fraser-

Shaw to the cult would vanish. So he decided to play "hero" and save Mike's life by shooting Dibela.

And it had almost worked.

"What I don't understand is how you knew the consul general was lying about being held captive," Kelly said.

"Noticed his wrist when he was holding the gun," I told her. "If he'd been bound and had struggled to free himself, the skin would have been chafed and raw. It wasn't. And that white summer suit of his—not a wrinkle or smudge on it. So I knew he had to be lying."

Kelly shook her head. "I still can't figure out why a man like Sir Leslie would involve himself in a blood cult."

"He was more than just involved," said Mike. "We got a full confession out of him. He was the guy behind the whole thing."

The three of us were in the Valley, sitting at a table at Jennifer's, another Aussie joint Kelly had discovered in Woodland Hills.

"That's right," I told her. "Fraser-Shaw began all this out of personal guilt. He felt the Aussies had mistreated the natives, including the ones in Papua New Guinea. Tribal cultures had been disrupted and destroyed. Then he found out about this core group from Papua. They'd immigrated to Los Angeles after independence. He began working with their leader, Renagi Dibela, to restore the ancient tribal customs. Even financed the building of the ceremonial house. But the situation got out of hand with the reversion to cannibalism."

"Yet he went along with it?" Kelly asked.

Mike nodded. "The creep admitted to us that he actually began to *enjoy* that aspect of it. Gave him a real power lift. And damned if he didn't *eat* part of those missing hearts!"

"Oh, wow!" said Kelly with a grimace.

"Couldn't have tasted worse than Vegemite," I said. She

gave me a dirty look.

"Private joke," I told Mike.

Lucero stood up. "Well, I gotta split. Lots of paperwork waiting for me at the station." He looked down at Kelly and me. "Like I said before, you guys make a handsome couple!"

And, with a wide grin, he left the restaurant.

"Mike's an incurable romantic," I told Kelly. "Since my divorce, he's been trying to link me up with the right woman."

"I've got a great idea," said Kelly.

"What's that?"

"Let's go to your place and link up."

She was right. It *did* turn out to be a great idea.

TWO

HELLHUNT

Night. A victim...terrified...alone...

She lay sprawled back against the cold stone, naked, her chilled flesh quivering, eyes wide, nostrils distended, her breath chopped and ragged. She pulled the fetid air into her gasping mouth, expelling it in broken, bubbling sounds.

She was an animal brought to slaughter; her young flesh would be torn and devoured—muscle, joint, tendon—chewed to raw bone, and the flowing product of her veins would slake a dark thirst.

She was alone. Trapped. Vulnerable. Beyond help, beyond hope.

Then she heard them coming for her.

And screamed.

1

I raised my head at the sound. The gull's sharp cry had broken through my meditation. A screaming wedge of birds wheeled above me, then winged off across the darkening water.

I stood up, brushing sand from my pants. Time to head home. I shook out my blanket, began folding it.

A mild breeze was flowing inland from the Pacific, making the waves restless, and the sun, like a magician's gold coin, had vanished below the wide horizon of water. The sand still retained the heat of the day (it was August), and was warm against my bare feet as I trudged back to my parked car.

My little red CRX Honda waited for me like a faithful dog at the edge of the Coastal Highway. In our totally mobile society of Southern California, cars are much more than transportation; they're a way of life.

I drove up Malibu Canyon, to Las Virgenes, and reached road's end near the Cottontail Ranch. The phone was ringing when I unlocked the front door. I picked it up. "Yo."

"David?" Kelly Rourke's velvet voice, tinged with annoyance.

"Who else would it be?"

"Why can't you just say hello like ordinary people?"

"I'm not ordinary people. You should know that by now."

Kelly is by way of being my girl. Nothing heavy. No engagement or wedding plans. But we seem to be drifting into a relationship that might or might not lead somewhere. Neither of us is in a hurry.

"Anything on for tonight?" she asked me.

"It's Tuesday," I said. "We're not suppose to get together till Friday."

"You didn't answer the question."

"I planned to slave over a hot word processor," I told her. "The final draft of *We're All Psychic* is a month overdue. And I was late with the last book."

"It can wait another day. I just got invited to a press preview in Westwood for *Demons by Darkness* and I need a hand to squeeze in the gross-out scenes."

I groaned. "You know how much I hate horror movies. They're stupid."

"This one's a DeMarco. He acts in only one film a year, and they're all a smash."

"De-who?"

"Alexander DeMarco. C'mon, even *you*—"

"The Sultan of Slice 'n' Dice. Yeah, I know. Stephen King's favorite actor."

"Precisely. And when DeMarco makes a fright flick it's big news. I'm getting an exclusive on this from the *Times*. Their regular reviewer is out with a flu bug. C'mon, David, give it a shot. Might turn out to be a classic."

"Okay, okay—but fair warning lady. I haven't liked a horror movie since Janet Leigh took her shower in *Psycho*."

"Kincaid, you're turning into a damn curmudgeon."

She never calls me Kincaid unless she's pissed.

2

Demons By Darkness was no classic. In fact, aside from some neat special effects and a bravura performance from DeMarco, it was mostly big budget nonsense. But I had to hand it to DeMarco; when he was on the screen you couldn't take your eyes off him. And despite a plethora of exploding vampires and dancing demons, he made the film come to life. The silly plot didn't matter. All that mattered was Alex DeMarco.

In the lobby of the Village Theater, while I waited by the door, Kelly buttonholed the film's producer, Lucas Appleton, for some quotes. I didn't pay much attention to what they were saying to each other until Appleton walked over to me. Appleton was a big, florid-faced man in Bugle Boy jeans, Reeboks, and a $400 Italian silk shirt from Rodeo Drive. And I'd be willing to bet the gold chain around his thick neck probably cost three times what the shirt did. He was wearing mirrored glasses, so I couldn't see his eyes, but I had the feeling he was sizing me up.

"So you're David Kincaid," he said, without shaking hands.

"Kelly here tells me you're an investigator."

"Of sorts," I said. "I work in the paranormal field. Teach, write, hold seminars, conduct consultations...that kind of thing. Investigation is part of it."

He handed me his card. "You'll do. Be at my office at ten tomorrow morning."

And he walked off.

I stared at the card, then at Kelly. "What was *that* all about?"

"He's a very abrupt man," she said. "But he obviously wants to hire you."

"For what?"

"How should I know? Go see him and find out."

3

I did. Mainly out of curiosity—to discover what one of the film industry's top producers wanted from me. Maybe he had a crazed poltergeist haunting his kitchen.

Universal Studios is in Burbank, cheek by jowl to Warners. The valley smog was taking a coffee break, so you could breathe without wearing a gas mask; it can get pretty murky in Burbank.

The gate guard looked like Sylvester Stallone. Tall and chunky. He gave me a hard look and checked my name against his clipboard. Then he smiled. "Righto, Mr. Kincaid. It's that big green building on the right, just past the water tower. Mr. Appleton's on the second floor."

"Which office?"

"It's *all* Appleton Productions," he said.

Which figured. When you swing the weight Lucas Appleton does in this town you don't get offices, you get *floors*.

"Mr. Appleton is in Projection Room C," a pert blonde at the reception desk told me. "He's expecting you."

I checked my watch. Three to ten. At least I was on time. I walked down a hall flanked with framed photos of Appleton's stars, the major talents he'd worked with through the years, and stopped in front of Alex DeMarco. He was standing at the door of a fake castle (cobwebs courtesy of the production department), a blood-stained ax in his hand, scowling at the camera, head lowered to accent his dark eyes. They were menacing and intense, reminding me of another horror great, Boris Karloff. When I was a kid at the movies, whenever old Boris leveled those piercing eyes at me, I'd cringe in the seat. DeMarco has The Look.

I continued on to Projection Room C at the far end of the hall. Easing open the door, I stepped inside. A film was being screened, but I couldn't see a damn thing in the darkness.

"Come ahead, Kincaid," a voice directed. "I'm three rows down."

I moved forward, fumbling like a blind man. As my eyes began adjusting to the reflected light from the screen, I saw Lucas Appleton sitting in the exact middle of an otherwise empty row of seats. He was the only one in the room.

"Sit," he told me. No greeting. No handshake. Like Kelly had said, an abrupt man. I took the seat next to him.

"I'm running a real piece of crapola," he said, gesturing toward the screen. "All about these no-brain teenagers trapped in the basement of a collapsed office building after an earthquake. Called *Deadly Earth*. It's deadly, all right."

"Is the picture one of yours?" I asked.

"You gotta be kidding! I make *quality* stuff. You saw *Demons by Darkness*." He snorted. "This waste of celluloid never deserved to get released."

Appleton stripped the cellophane from a long thin cigar and sighed deeply, sticking the cigar in the right corner of his mouth. "Gave up smoking," he said. "I don't like these. Just use 'em as pacifiers."

I didn't say anything to that.

"We're coming to the part of this turkey I wanted you to see. Watch for the kid in the background. Young girl. Her leg is supposed to be caught under a fallen beam...ah, *there* she is—the groaning kid in the ripped blouse." He leaned over an intercom, popped a switch. "Freeze it, Sid."

The projectionist in the booth behind us locked the girl's image in place on the screen.

"What about her?"

"Take a good look. Get her fixed in your head. This was made about three years ago, so she'd be fifteen. She's eighteen by now. Name's Justina Phillips. She's not registered with the Guild or repped by an agent, so maybe this was just a one-shot for her."

I stared at the frozen image of the dark-haired teenager. "So...what's this got to do with me?"

Instead of replying, the producer hit the intercom switch again. "Lights, Sid."

I blinked as the overheads went on.

Appleton stood up. "Follow me," he said.

We walked out of the projection room and down another side hall to his office. It was the size of Grand Central Station. But rather starkly furnished. A giant wall poster of *Demons by Darkness* filled most of the wall behind an iceberg-white desk.

He stood by the desk, nodding toward the poster. "So... what do you think? I personally designed it myself. Told the artist just what to paint. Classy, eh?"

Under the film's main title, a drooling purple demon with wild red eyes was perched on the stomach of a terrified girl who'd been chained to a table. He had a glittering knife raised, ready to cut her throat. Another demon, also purple, was directly behind her, puling her head back by the hair to bare the vulnerable white arc of her neck.

Hovering over the scene were the ghostly white eyes of Alex DeMarco, his face shining from background darkness.

FIENDS! FREAKS! FLESH EATERS!
APPLETON PRODUCTIONS PRESENTS
THE SCREEN'S REIGNING
MONARCH OF TERROR...
DEMARCO!
IN A FILM OF
FURY, FEAR, AND FASCINATION

"I thought up all those 'F' words," declared Appleton. "It's called alliteration when you do that."

"Yeah, I know. I do a little writing myself."

"So what do you think?"

"Very...classy," I said, knowing that was what he wanted to hear.

Appleton settled into a tall scoop-backed cream-colored leather chair behind the desk, shifting the unlit cigar to the left side of his mouth. "So you want to know what *you* have to do with Justina Phillips?"

"Is that her real name?"

"Yes. I checked." He slid open a drawer, reached inside for a manila envelope, and thrust it across the white desk at me.

"It's all there. Everything I could find out about her. Along with an 8 x 10 glossy I had blown up from the frame. But like I said, she's three years older now."

"So?"

"So she has definite potential. Great eyes, sensuous mouth, a special look. I could build her into a star. But first, of course, I need to find her. That's what I'm hiring you for."

I shook my head. "You've got the wrong boy," I told him.

"I'm no detective, I'm an investigator in the field of the paranormal. That's a long way from a private eye. I don't find lost teenagers."

He ignored this. "I had her last known address checked in Santa Monica. She's not there anymore. Called her parents, and they have no clue where she is—don't know, don't care. Haven't laid eyes on her since she left home at fifteen right after doing the bit part in *Deadly Earth*."

"That's pretty young," I said. "To leave home at that age, you'd think her parents would be going nuts with no contact."

"Anyhow..." continued Appleton, "we got zip on where Justina is now. Gonna be up to you."

"I told you—I'm not the one for this."

"Even for a five thousand cash retainer? Plus a fat bonus if you find her."

"You've talked me into it." I grinned. "But why not hire a licensed private detective?"

"I'm a man of instinct," he said, flipping the well-chewed cigar into a snaptop desk tray. "And my instinct tells me you're right for this job." He stood up and walked around the desk to clap me on the shoulder. "Do we understand one another?"

"I think we do," I said.

I left Universal Studios carrying the manila envelope.

And five thousand dollars of Lucas Appleton's money tucked snugly away in my wallet.

4

Over lunch at Hollywood at Musso & Frank's (they make great au gratin potatoes), I studied the material inside the envelope. There wasn't much. Clipped to Justina's photo, an

actor's pay sheet for *Deadly Earth*, signed by her. A printed transcript of a radio talk show in which she plugged the
pic between dog food commercials. And a very brief list of
known contacts. These included the director who worked
with her on the film, and the studio flack who got her the radio bit spot—plus her parents, Mr. and Mrs. Edwin G. Phillips. They lived in San Diego.

Took me the rest of the afternoon to get down there and
find their place—an impressive two-story ranch style home
on a quiet cul de sac near Balboa Park.

Mrs. Phillips answered the door.

She was as tall as I am, just under six feet—but she
carried her weight with poise. Cool gray eyes. Hair as neatly
trimmed as the box hedge on her porch. Dressed in a mint
green slacks-and-blouse combo you don't get at a Sears sale.
A small, perfectly cut diamond mounted in gold at her throat
was modestly impressive. Mrs. Phillips personified what
Lucas Appleton thought his poster had: class.

She'd been expecting a salesman from some insurance
company, and when she found out I wasn't him, it took some
fast talk to get me invited inside.

"I *told* those people at the studio I don't have any idea
where my daughter is," she said in a voice as cool as her
eyes.

We were seated on a large studio couch in the Phillips'
living room. Late afternoon sun had turned the drapes to
gold flame, and a spear of sunlight illumined a large framed
photo on the grand piano. Mr. and Mrs. Phillips, posed
hand-in-hand.

"I understand you can't supply information you don't
have," I said in my I'm-really-a-nice-fellow voice. "I was
hoping you could direct me to someone who might know
where she is. Maybe a boyfriend?"

"If Justina has a boyfriend, it's no concern of mine," she

said stiffly. "I have no leads for you, Mr. Kincaid, and I regret the inconvenience of your trip."

That would have ended it—but I decided to take a wild shot. "Just when did you and your husband adopt Justina?"

She flushed, stood up, staring at me. "How did you know about that?"

I walked over and picked up the framed photo from the piano, studying it. "This photograph of you and Mr. Phillips—and the one I have of Justina—there's absolutely no family resemblance. Everything's different. Eyes, nose, the shape of the chin—everything."

She crossed to a heavy brass-studded chair and sat down on it, looking pale. "We adopted Justina shortly after her birth at St. Joseph's Hospital. She was...born out of wedlock. Her birth parents weren't married."

"Did you tell her she was adopted?"

"Yes, but not until her fifteenth birthday. She was furious with us for what she termed 'withholding the truth.' She packed and left the same day." Mrs. Phillips looked down at her hands; her face was set, unforgiving. "We have not seen her since."

"No contact at all?"

"A letter last Christmas, requesting money. She listed a post office box as an address."

"What did you do about the letter?"

"We destroyed it. My husband and I feel that Justina has acted in a most ungrateful manner. We gave her clothes, a good home, a solid education—and she rejected us."

"Did you give her love?"

Mrs. Phillips looked up at me. Then, slowly: "We tried to. Edwin and I are not emotional people."

A moment of awkward silence. Then: "Do you know the name of her birth mother?"

"On the certificate it was 'Leona Stoddard.' I have no idea

if that was her real name. Frankly, I have no interest in the woman."

"What made you adopt Justina?"

"It was Edwin. We were childless—but Edwin wanted to be a father. Heaven knows why, since he never had any time for Justina. Personally, I never wanted a child."

I looked into those cool gray eyes. "I guess that's pretty obvious," I said.

5

After I left the Phillips house, I took a long chance and drove to St. Joseph's Hospital where Justina had been born; it was in the suburb of Chula Vista. I had a strong desire to see if anyone at the place remembered her birth eighteen years ago.

All hospitals look alike, smell alike, sound alike; St. Joseph's was no exception. Only difference: this one was staffed by nuns.

I got lucky. The nun who'd been on floor duty at the time of Justina's birth was still on staff. Sister Irma.

When we sat down in the patients' reception area, she reminded me of an undersized Santa Claus: just five feet, but fat and jolly, with twinkling eyes. She looked about fifty.

"I've always loved working around babies," she told me, hands tucked primly away inside her wide sleeves of an old-fashioned nun's habit. "If the Good Lord hadn't called me to His service, I would have mothered a large family. But then..." And she twinkled. "...*all* the babies I've taken care of through the years are mine. Silly, I suppose, yet I can't help thinking of them that way. But then, aren't we all part of God's greater family?"

"And you *do* remember the Stoddard baby?"

She nodded. "Indeed I do. A lovely little thing—like one of God's angels."

"Do you recall what her mother was like?"

Suddenly the brightness vanished from her face. Her eyes darkened. "Yes...I do remember the woman," she said softly. "It's a blessing she never raised that poor child."

"What makes you say that?"

"She had true *evil* in her, Mr. Kincaid," declared Sister Irma. "Her eyes...they were...quite horrible. There is a perfect word to fit them: demonic."

"And the baby's father?"

"I don't recall his name," she said, "but I know that he drove a cab in the San Diego area. He visited the hospital only once, when I attempted to stir his conscience, asking him why he had not married the mother of this child."

"What did he say?"

"He told me it was none of my business. I got very angry, may the Good Lord forgive me, and followed him out to his cab, shouting at him." She looked as if she were still feeling the guilt of this act eighteen years later. "I watched him drive away and I have always remembered the number of his taxi. It was 636—a Star Cab vehicle."

She sat stiffly, drained of good humor by the memory.

"Did you personally care for the baby?"

"Oh, yes. I took a special interest in her. Whenever I was on duty I'd see to her first. Never gave me any worry. An absolute angel. After they took her away, I found out she'd been put up for adoption. And that's the last I heard of her." She looked at me in sudden concern. "Is the dear girl all right?"

"I hope so. Her name is Justina Phillips—and I'm trying to locate her for a job." I stood up. "You've been very kind, Sister. I appreciate your talking to me."

"I'm curious, Mr. Kincaid."

"About what?"

"Why did you come *here*?"

"I wanted to talk with someone who'd actually seen her birth mother. Thought I might find out more about Leona Stoddard. If I could find her, she might lead me to Justina. They *could* be back in touch. That often happens with adopted children."

The nun paled; she lowered her eyes. "If you ever *do* come face to face with that awful woman..." Her lower lip quivered. "...may God protect you!"

And Sister Irma hastily made the Sign of the Cross.

6

The Star Cab Company was near the Coast Highway, at the bottom of Grand in downtown San Diego. I'd be getting there after dark.

On the way, I kept thinking of how it must feel to grow up in a loveless environment.

For Justina, once her birth mother abandoned her, she never found love. Mrs. Phillips had made it clear that she lacked any kind of emotional tie to the girl—and her busy husband obviously didn't either. They didn't give a damn for their daughter. No wonder she took off on her own at fifteen; discovering she was no blood relative to the Phillips freed her to go.

Had she attempted to locate her birth mother or father?

What kind of emotional state was she in?

Was she, for that matter, still alive?

A Navy town, San Diego was big during the Second World War. As a port city, it got a lot of wear and tear, and the downtown area became seedy and unattractive. Until the City Council voted for a major face lift—ugly to beautiful.

San Diego's city fathers can be proud of the job they've done with the new downtown area. All big cities should look so good.

I parked the Honda behind Star's red brick office-and-garage, walked in and asked to see the owner.

"Hey, Harl!" yelled a beefy mechanic working on one of the cabs. "Somebody's here to see ya."

Harl waddled out of his glass-walled office, fat as a spider, wearing a greasy pair of white overalls a size too small for him. "I'm Harley Pike. What can I do for you?"

I'd gotten the name of Justina's father from the hospital, so I knew who to ask for. "I'm trying to locate a driver of yours, Al Devits. Worked here in '73."

"That's a long time back," said Pike, scrubbing at his cheek with black-nailed fingers. "I wasn't around in those days. Long time back."

"Can't you check your records?"

"I guess," he said, and sighed. "Come on back to the office and I'll see if I got something on this guy. D-E-V-I-T-S, is it?"

"Right." I trailed him to his office at the far end of the garage. It was like Pike—overloaded and greasy.

He blew the dust off a yellowed record book, opened it, thumbing through the entries. "Yeah...here he is...Albert A. Devits. Drove for us into '75." He looked up at me. "You want his address back then? It's a forwarding—from where he moved from here." He hesitated. "Here's a photo of him. We got no use for it."

"Great," I said.

The address: a small apartment in a pink stucco building behind what used to be the old MGM Studios in Culver City. It was late when I got to the place, and I hoped I wasn't getting anybody out of bed. I wasn't. The guy who answered my ring was Al himself. He was watching the midnight news on TV.

Devits told me he'd been living here since he moved up from San Diego in the fall of '75. He was in his mid-fifties, with a lean, acne-pocked face and sad eyes, like a beagle. He looked worn and defeated. An ashtray overflowing with dead cigarette butts told me he was a chain smoker.

"I don't do no work of any kind these days," he told me in a smoke-fogged voice as we sat facing one another in his small living room. He tapped his right leg. "Fake," he said, smiling. His teeth were tobacco-stained. "Lost the real one in the service. I live on a vet's pension."

"Sorry," I said.

"Don't be. I'm fine. I live okay." He got out a fresh pack of Camels. "Mind if I smoke?"

"I'd rather you wouldn't."

"Okay." And he put away the cigarettes.

"I came here to ask about your child."

"Got no children." He grunted. "Never married."

"I'm talking about the baby girl Leona Stoddard delivered at St. Joseph's in 1973."

"Oh *that*," he said. His voice was raspy, like a file on wood. "I try not to do any thinkin' about that."

"You know anything about what happened to her?"

He shifted, leaning forward to adjust his right leg. "Mister, I never seen that kid but once. For maybe five minutes in the hospital. Don't know nothin' about her. Don't want to. Her mother...was bad enough."

"What do you mean?"

"I mean that woman gave me the willies, just bein' around her. Somethin' wrong with her."

"In what way?"

"Dunno exactly. Just...that she wasn't *natural*. I got no words for it."

"Did you see her again after the birth of the baby?"

"Hell, no! Never!" Devits shuddered. "I made a mistake mixin' with her in the first place. But she had...funny eyes. She could look at you...and it was like you were..."

"Hypnotized?"

"Yeah, that's it, hypnotized. Eyes like hers—you don't forget."

"Do you have a photo of her?"

He got up, favoring his bad leg, limped to a shelf, and removed a shoe box. Opened it and got out a photo.

"That's Leona," he said, handing it me. "See what I mean?"

Even though it was only a 5 x 7 snapshot, Leona Stoddard's eyes seemed to burn out of the photo, intense and darkly lustrous. She looked about twenty-five with full, sensual lips and a mass of dark hair framing the pale oval of her face. Striking. And definitely the mother of Justina Phillips. In black ink, on the bottom strip of the photo, she had scrawled, "Yours, Leona."

"I took that picture myself a week after we met. That's the whole time we were together—that week back in '72. Didn't see her again till she got to the hospital. I went over to get me a look at the baby, but I couldn't see anythin' of me in the kid. She had Leona's hair and eyes. I saw her, and then I left. And I haven't seen either of 'em since."

"How did you and Leona first meet?"

"In my cab. She called from the U.S. Grant Hotel in downtown San Diego. I picked her up outside the hotel to take her somewhere... The next thing I know— we're in the sack together."

"Did she have some kind of job in those days?"

"Not that I knew about. I remember she said she was an actress. In the movies. But I wouldn't know about that. I never go to no movies."

"Mind if I keep this photo?"

"You're welcome to it. I don't want to look at that face of hers...ever again."

As I was leaving I asked Al Devits one final question: "I can understand your feelings for Leona—but aren't you curious about what happened to your daughter?"

"She don't exist far as I'm concerned," he said. "I don't want nothin' to do with *anythin'* that come out of Leona Stoddard."

The next day I spent some time accessing files of the Academy of Motion Picture Arts and Sciences in Beverly Hills.

There was no separate listing for "Stoddard, Leona," but in a book of film history I ran across what I was *certain* was a photo of her. The actress was languishing in the arms of Rudolph Valentino in a tent setting for one of his desert love sagas.

Same face. Same dark hair. Same arresting, intense eyes. But the caption named her as "Louise Collins"—and the film was a silent, made back in the 1920s when Valentino was the rage. If Lousie Collins and Leona Stoddard *had* been the same woman, she'd have been in her seventies when Al met her.

And that didn't make sense.

7

"Could be Louise Collins was Leona's mother," Kelly said over dinner that night in a booth at Musso's. She was comparing the snapshot of Leona with a Xerox copy of the photo from the Valentino film.

"I checked that angle," I told her. "Louise Collins died in a plane crash in 1930. Never married. No kids."

She handed the photos back to me. "Leona *could* have been illegitimate—same as *her* daughter."

"Maybe." I shook my head. "But anyone would swear they're the same woman. How could she be an identical twin to her mother?"

"Happens all the time. My younger sister looks almost exactly like Mom did at her age."

"Well, it doesn't matter now. I'm giving up on Leona Stoddard. I need to move in a new direction. Justina's parents are obviously not going to help me find her."

"Then what *are* you going to do?" Kelly asked. She looked terrific. Her hair was combed back in a low ponytail fastened with a black satin bow. She was wearing more makeup than usual—violet eye shadow for one more thing—and on her it looked great. Kelly's tight green dress matched her eyes. She looked every bit as good as any of the actresses sitting in the booths around us. I realized that I'd been neglecting her; we hadn't made love in more than a week.

"I'll tell you what I'm going to do. I'm going to drive you home, lock the car, and spend the night in your apartment." I grinned at her. "How does that sound?"

"Sounds like a deal." And she grinned back at me.

8

Next morning, I phoned Lucas Appleton at the studio, telling him that so far I'd had no luck in tracing Justina, but I was determined to keep trying. (After all, it was *his* money.)

"You stay right on this, Kincaid," he told me. "I'll be leaving tomorrow for Oregon. Three days. I'll be back by Tuesday."

"Hopefully by then, I'll have better news for you."

"Contact me Tuesday morning," he said. "It's vital I find this girl."

I put down the phone thoughtfully. What was so "vital" about finding an unknown bit player who may or may not have enough talent to make it in films?

That was when I began to suspect that there was more involved here than screen acting.

But *what*?

I figured it was time to use one of my paranormal contacts. I happen to believe we're all psychic, to an extent, but that some people possess this talent to a much great degree than others.

I decided to consult a professional.

Naturally, as with any profession, there are phonies. I've encountered (and unmasked) a lot of them in my business. However, Irene Hopwood was genuine. I'd made use of her particular talents in the past, and was convinced she had powers far beyond the ordinary.

She worked out of a lovingly renovated Victorian house in downtown Los Angeles, one of those tall, ornate gingerbread-and-stained-glass jobs that used to crowd the Bunker Hill area before most of them were torn down to make room for big-bucks condos.

Her office was on the lower floor, facing the street.

Irene saw people only by appointment—and I'd made one. For that night, at 10 p.m. (She was never at her best by daylight and claimed that darkness aided her psychic powers.)

"David! How very nice to see you again!" Tasteful jewelry glittered on her fingers and wrist as she extended her hand to me. I pressed it warmly.

"Been a while," I said.

"Please, come in." She led me inside to an old-fashioned parlor. A pot of Earl Grey tea and a plate of big cookies (she knew I loved chocolate chip) were laid out on an antique table.

I made small talk as we sat down. Then, sipping her tea and munching a chocolate chip cookie, I got around to what had brought me there.

"I'm looking for a young woman. Eighteen. Name's Justina Phillips." I opened my leather briefcase, handed over the 8 x 10 glossy Appleton had given me.

She studied the image. "Arresting eyes," she murmured. "Quite intense." Then she looked up at me. "Do you have an object of hers—a ring, or a bracelet perhaps?"

"No," I said. "I was hoping you could home in on the name and face and come up with something—maybe get a mental image of her present whereabouts."

She stared at the photo, closed her eyes, softly repeating: "Justina...Justina...Justina..."

I leaned forward. "Anything?"

Slowly, she shook her head. "Nothing. As you know, my own talents work mainly through psychometry. To receive the most accurate vibrations, I need an object owned by the subject, preferably something the subject has worn or otherwise touched a lot. Photos which have been handled by the subject *can* carry vibrational auras, but I'm not receiving any from this one."

"She never touched this," I said.

"Well, then, I'm going to need more. An item of her clothing...something *tangible*."

I reached into my briefcase, took out the signed snapshot of Leona Stoddard, gave it to her. "Try this. It's a photo of her mother."

"Yes. I can see that in the eyes...so powerfully intense." Irene traced her fingers slowly over the face in the snapshot. Then, as if it were white hot, she pulled back abruptly, allowing the picture to slip to the polished wood floor.

I picked it up. "What's wrong?"

Her breathing was rapid and shallow; she sat rigidly in the chair, hands fisted. "I feel a...terrible darkness in this individual...a sense of perversion...of *foulness!*" She stood up. "I'm blocked. That's all I can give you."

I didn't question her reaction, but it disturbed me.

I returned Leona's snapshot to my briefcase. "I may be back," I said.

At the door, Irene gripped my arm. I could feel the strength of her fingers. "A warning, David. There is...a force here...powerful and horrific. You're moving toward it—and it can destroy you."

Her words had definitely shaken me.

By the time I was back inside the Honda, fumbling for the ignition key, I found that my hands were moist with cold sweat.

9

I was tired, very tired as I reached the end of Las Virgenes Road. I wanted nothing more than a good night's sleep to clear my head, to give my conscious mind a period of quiet restoration.

As I rolled the CRX into the gravel driveway fronting my house I saw something move just at the edge of my vision. Something in the yard, among the trees. A dark mass, shifting ominously.

I stopped, cutting the Honda's engine. Silence. Just the throbbing dirge of crickets. The darkness pressed in thickly around me like a stifling shroud.

Since I live in a remote, semi-wilderness area, the intruder could well be a night animal—perhaps a prowling mountain lion. If so, he'd be more afraid of me than I'd be of him. Best to make sure.

As I was reaching for my flashlight in the glove compartment, I saw a pair of eyes, red and luminous, glowing from the shadows.

They moved closer.

I clicked on the flash, swinging the arc of light toward the intruder. And gasped. My beam illuminated the stark, oval face of Leona Stoddard, lips pulled back in a snarl, eyes hot and probing. Her hair was tangled and filth-matted.

Horribly, incredibly, only her *face* was human! The lower part of her body, glistening wetly in the powdery beam of light, was that of an enormous insect—and its multiple legs, like those of a giant centipede, began to propel it rapidly toward the car.

Panic and revulsion welled through me. I snaplocked the door, desperately keying the ignition. The engine sputtered and died. I tried again.

Too late. The thing had reached my side of the Honda and now its plated insect legs were scrabbling at the window. Powerfully, they smashed at the glass which gave way in falling shards, exposing me to the bloated horror outside.

"You are *mine!*" hissed the Leona-thing, dipping her head through the shattered window to fasten razor teeth in my right shoulder. I screamed in shock and pain as, shark-like, she ripped away a gouting chunk of my flesh.

I slammed the metal flashlight against her head, but the blow had no effect.

Ripping free of her, blood erupting from my savaged shoulder, I threw myself across the seat to dive out the passenger door.

Landing on my knees in the sharp gravel, I lunged up, began running for the dark bulk of the house.

The Leona-thing scrambled spider-quick over the top of the Honda and launched itself at me. Its loathesome body struck my back, slamming me to the ground. I twisted around, throwing both arms across my face.

Again, the evil hiss of Leona's voice: "*Mine!*"

And her slashing teeth severed my left arm at the elbow;

the whole lower portion, hand, wrist, and forearm—gone! As a welter of crimson cloaked my body, I watched, in numb horror, as she devoured my flesh, snapping the bones of my fingers like breadsticks.

I closed my eyes, my nostrils filled with the sharp, metallic insect odor of the Leona-thing...

I sat up, blinking, shaking wildly, saliva running from my open mouth. Sweat, not blood, soaked my face and chest.

What a nightmare!

I knew I was all right, safe and unharmed, in my own bedroom, with an early, pale-rose sunrise staining the lower edge of the sky outside the window—but the horrific demon figure of Leona Stoddard had been so vivid and tactile that I found it difficult to believe I was still alive.

And I'd analyzed enough dreams to know that this one was a warning.

10

A few hours later, a telephone call put me back on Justina's trail.

It was Mrs. Phillips phoning from San Diego to tell me she thought that perhaps Bobbi Graham might be able to help me in my search.

"Who's he?" I asked.

"Graham is a female," said Mrs. Phillips, her voice tight and strained. "Justina was...involved with her. I was ashamed to tell you."

"Involved? You mean sexually?"

"Oh no, nothing like that." A hesitation on the line. "It's...a drug thing."

"Tell me about it."

"After she dropped out of school, Justina got in with a bad

crowd. She became close friends with this Graham girl, and it was Bobbi Graham who introduced her to hard drugs."

"How hard is hard?"

"Cocaine mostly—and some others I don't know about. And she didn't just decide to go off on her own; we *asked* her to leave. Demanded it, really. The psychologists call the process 'Tough Love.' So she went to Los Angeles with the Graham girl. I'm sure they lived there together."

"That would figure, at her age."

"When you asked about Justina...well I didn't want to get into this drug problem. I trust you'll understand."

"I *do*—and I appreciate your calling me."

"If Justina can get an acting career started for herself, then I don't want to stand in her way," she said firmly. "I may not love her in a conventional sense, Mr. Kincaid, but I do care about her welfare."

"Do you have an address for Bobbi Graham?"

She did.

In Venice.

I drove there.

11

Venice has the reputation of being a "doper's heaven." You can get anything from rock cocaine to ice—the latest mind-blaster—on the streets of Venice, so from what Mrs. Phillips has told me, I wasn't surprised Bobbi Graham lived here.

Originally, emulating the grand Italian city that had inspired it, Venice had been designed as a graceful community of sparkling canals (with gondolas yet!) trim green lawns, immaculate streets, and bright-painted pastel houses. That was a long time ago. Now it was worth your life to be caught there on certain streets after dark. The canals were scummed and rancid (you could smell them all the way to Wilshire), filled with rusty water and floating debris best left undescribed.

Bobbi Graham was renting a small, weather-wracked frame house between one of the canals and the ocean, an eyesore among eyesores.

I got out of the Honda and walked across the blistered weed patch that had once been a front yard and knocked on a paint-chipped screen door.

Bobbi was waiting for me, as she'd promised. I heard her voice from inside. "Walk in. The door's open."

I stepped into a cramped, trash-littered living room. Bobbi was slouched in a sagging, near-colorless sofa (it had once been orange), watching television with a sleepy black cat in her lap. The cat regarded me with slitted, smoke-yellowed eyes, yawned hugely, then went back to sleep.

Bobbi lifted the animal from her lap and got up to switch off the TV. Aside from assorted trash, the faded sofa, a single wooden kitchen chair, and the TV set were the only items in the room.

"I was watching Geraldo," she said. "Ever watch his show?"

"I was on it once, but no, I can't say that I *watch* it," I said.

Her eyes took on new life. To most people, anybody who's been on television is a celebrity.

"He rounds up some really freaky people. Like, just before you got here, he was interviewing a defrocked priest who owns a string of condom factories in the East. Guy was a real kick."

Bobbi had flopped back on the sofa and I took the chair. She was barefoot, in ragged jeans and a beaded shirt with most of the beads missing. Her face was pinched and narrow-boned, with small bloodshot eyes. She wore no makeup, and her greased, pasty skin was proof that she needed to improve her diet.

"Just who *are* you anyway?" she asked me.

"I'm an independent investigator."

"You mean like a cop? If you're a cop, I don't do drugs anymore, so you're wasting your time."

I smiled at that. I'm no cop. I work in the field of the paranormal."

"Like ghosts and stuff?"

"That's part of it."

"Then why are you nosing around after Justina? She's no ghost."

"I'm glad to hear that."

"Well...*why* then?"

"I just need to find her. Personal reasons."

She narrowed her eyes, then smiled. Bobbi had a nice smile; it softened her face, brightened it.

"You're kinda cute. How old are you?"

"Thirty-one."

"I'm twenty. Guess that maybe makes you too old for me." She shrugged. "Okay...so what do you want to ask me about Justina?"

"Do you know where she is now?"

"Nope. She *was* living here with me, until about three months ago, but we had us a fight, so she split." Bobbi picked up the cat again, began stroking its charcoal back.

"What was the fight about?"

"You *sure* you're not a cop?"

"Swear to God."

"Okay...it was about doing drugs. She wanted to quit. Claimed they were bumming her out. Thought maybe she was losing her mind."

"So did she quit?"

"I guess so. She went to this rehab house in Hollywood to get help. That's where she met Lyle."

"Who's Lyle?"

"A guy who worked there. Maybe he still does. Lyle Anmar. She told me they had a thing going for a while, but I dunno if it lasted. Maybe you should ask Lyle."

I nodded. "Maybe I should. Got an address for the place?"

"It's somewhere on Western, near Hollywood Boulevard. Called 'The New Beginning.' Justina phoned me from there a couple of times."

"I'll find it."

The cat jumped down from her lap and came over to rub against my leg. "He likes me," I said.

"He's just hungry. Thinks you'll feed him. Homer's a real glutton. Eats all time. I'm gettin' a beer. Want one?"

"No thanks."

She went into a small, grubby kitchen and fetched a Coors, popping the can and returning with it. "Last time Justina called from this place, she wanted me to come over and join some program they have. Get me clean. I told her to screw off. *That'll* be the friggin' day—when I go to some friggin' rehab house!"

"Then you still do drugs?"

"Yeah." She shrugged her thin shoulders. "Anyhow, that was the last time I heard from her. I don't know where she is now."

"One more thing," I said.

"What?"

"When she was here with you...did she ever talk about her mother? Her *birth* mother?"

"Only that she was pissed at being deserted, being put up for adoption the way she was. She figured her Mom had to be a primo bitch to do a thing like that."

"She ever show any interest in locating her real mother?"

"Not that I saw. She was too pissed at her."

"What about her life with the Phillips—was she happy when she was with them?"

"For while. She had this picture of a birthday party they gave for her down in San Diego at Balboa Park. When she turned ten. They hired a couple of clowns and even rented a kids' merry-go-round. She said that was the happiest day of her life."

"The picture—did she take it with her?"

"No. It's still around here with some of the other stuff she left. Wanta see it?"

"Yeah."

"Okay, if I can find it." She put her can of beer on the floor while she dug into a large cardboard box by the wall near the kitchen, pulling out various papers, shaking her head. Then she tried another box. This time she turned to me in triumph, holding up the photo. "Got it."

It was a color shot the size of a postcard. Young Justina was posed, smiling, between two clowns. She looked pink and healthy. I was about to hand it back when a figure caught my eye. A man. Standing behind them in the far background, staring toward the camera.

Somehow, he looked familiar, but I couldn't place him. The figure was too small and indistinct.

"Can I borrow this?"

"Promise to bring it back?"

"Promise."

As I was leaving, Bobbi stopped me. She looked haunted. "If you find Justina, tell her..." She hesitated, tears welling in her eyes. "Tell her I still love her."

"I'll tell her," I said.

12

In Hollywood I dropped off the picture at Professional Photo Processing, telling them I wanted a blowup...and what about enhancing the figure in the background? They said I could pick it up in the morning. To them, it was just another job.

I had no trouble finding the number of the rehab house in the Hollywood phone book. When I got them on the line they told me, yes, Lyle Anmar still worked the night shift there. Starting at eleven. I said I'd drop by before midnight.

The delay gave me time to catch a late dinner at Gorky's. Russian food, like Russian literature, leads to introspection. Alone with my thoughts, I realized that finding Justina Phillips had become a personal quest; I'd developed an emotional interest in the girl, a mix of curiosity and compassion. I found myself hoping she was all right, that the rehab people had provided the help she needed.

13

The New Beginning was on Western, just a block down from Hollywood Boulevard. A big rambling converted Span-ish-style apartment complex that had been a respectable enough address before this section of town had gone to seed. Now it was smack in the middle of a ghetto area, and its newly-painted turquoise exterior contrasted sharply with the dingy, dirt-encrusted buildings around it on the same block. Scrawled graffiti were everywhere in sweeping, bold patterns—street gangs marking their turf with spray paint the way cats mark their territory with scent.

Like Venice, not a great place to be caught after dark. But Lyle Anmar worked here and we needed to talk.

The door buzzer summoned a bent-backed old man with

maybe three strands of hair left on his freckled head. He blinked at me through bottle-thick glasses, running a rusty tongue over cracked lips. "Help ya, mister?"

"I was told that Lyle Anmar works the night shift. I'm here to see him."

"Then you best talk to Sylva. She's the one in charge. Don't know the young folks by name." He coughed raggedly. "Been a long time since I could remember names." He beckoned to me. "Step inside. I'll go fetch Sylva."

She was in her mid-twenties, dark and pretty. Her eyes were direct but weary; they'd seen a lot. "You the one who called about Lyle?"

I nodded. It was 11:30; I figured he'd be in. He was.

"In the rec room," she said. I followed her down a long, freshly-painted hall. She opened a door and we walked into a wide room crowded with video games, pinball machines, and faded pool tables. Three of the video games were in action. "He's the tall guy," said Sylva, and left me there.

Lyle was at one of the green tables, neatly sinking the eight ball into a corner pocket. He was at least six-three, rangy and raw-boned, with a thin blond beard and long hair tied behind in a ponytail. His opponent was a teenage girl in ragged slacks and a gray pullover. She looked nervous and strung out.

"Like to talk to you," I said to Lyle Anmar. "I'm David Kincaid."

"And I'm busy." He was chalking his cue stick as the girl took her turn. She didn't sink anything. I waited, watching him run the table, socking home the last three balls.

"Want another game?" he asked the girl.

"Not with you," she said. "I never win when I play with you." And she wandered off to one of the pinball machines.

Anmar racked his stick, then swung to face me. He seemed as tall as the Empire State Building, but a lot skinnier. "So what d'ya want to talk about?"

"Justina Phillips," I said.

"Buzz off." He reached for the leather jacket he'd draped over a chair.

"This is important," I said.

"Why should I talk to you?" His mouth was sullen, his eyes a frosted blue.

"If you think I'm a cop, you're wrong," I told him.

"I don't give a crap *who* you are." He started out of the room.

I stopped him at the door. "Talk to me, Lyle. You're the only lead I've got."

"To what?"

"To Justina. I need to find her. There's a chance she could get into films, make some really good money, have a decent life. If you care about her—"

"And what makes you think I do?"

"Bobbi Graham said that you and Justina were involved."

"That little skank don't know nothin' about me." His tone was as cold as his eyes.

"I thought you were here because you wanted to help people," I said, allowing sudden anger to color my voice.

"So?"

"So you may be able to help Justina. If you'll just talk to me about her."

He seemed to relax; his eyes softened. "Okay, mister. It just happens I *do* care about her, even if she doesn't care about me."

"She broke up with you?"

"Sure as hell did. Once she got her head straight she told me we were history."

"Then she's clean?"

"She was—when she left here," he said.

"You ever do drugs with her?"

"Not with her, I didn't. I was clean when I came here. In fact, I helped her get straight."

Two of the video game players were looking at us.

"Can we sit down somewhere?" I asked. "There's a lot more that I'd like to know."

"Yeah...all right. You want some coffee?"

I nodded. "Fine."

We sat down over coffee in a deserted kitchen area behind the rec room.

By now, Anmar had opened up; in fact, he seemed anxious to talk about his relationship with Justina. He said she'd come here because of what her dreams had done to her.

"That's how she got into drugs in the first place," Lyle said. "She told me she began using because she thought it might help her escape the nightmares. But it didn't help—just made the dreams worse."

"Did she say what they were about?"

"No. She didn't want to talk about them. But she did say one thing..."

"Yeah?"

"Said they were all weird. *Supernatural*, she said."

"You mean—ghosts?"

"Demons," Lyle told me. "Justina said a lot of them were about demons—but she wouldn't go into details. I know they were real bad, though. Scared her a lot." He hesitated. "But there was one thing I could never figure."

"What was that?"

"We have a VCR here—and she was always renting horror videos—all of the Alex DeMarco movies. She'd watch them over and over. I told her they were probably giving her the nightmares, but she said she had to watch them."

"*Had* to?"

"Like she was...*compelled* to do it. But she never said why. It was all pretty crazy."

I thought about that. Then I backtracked, asking him how he got hooked on drugs.

"I was riding with the Henchmen when it started," he said.

"The motorcycle gang?"

"Yes. They're a mean bunch, but for a while they were like...a family to me. But when I found out what they were into, I got out. I knew I had to get my head straight."

"What *are* they into?"

"A lot of stuff—but the worst, for me, was the girl thing. They supply young girls to local pimps. Pick up an out-of-town chick right off the bus, then sweet-talk her into riding with them. Find out she's on the run and can't be traced. Next thing you know, she's history. Gone. Like she never was."

"You know the names of the pimps they supply?"

"No. I was never into that part of it. And, like I say, when I found out what was going down, I split."

"Justina ever run with the gang?"

"No. Never. There's no connection."

I made a mental note to have my cop pal, Mike Lucero, check out the Henchmen. Then I asked: "Do you have any idea where Justina might be right now?"

He shook his head. "She could be anywhere. Or nowhere."

"Meaning?"

He looked at me. "How do we know she's still alive?"

"We don't," I said.

14

The next morning I picked up my enhanced birthday photo of Justina—and recognized the figure in the background of the shot.

Alex DeMarco.

It was just too coincidental—Justina's fascination with his films and then finding out that DeMarco had been at her tenth birthday party. Maybe he had something to do with what I now thought of as her "disappearance."

But first, before I could talk to him, I had to find his address. They don't list major film stars in the phone book.

I drove over to Murdock Studios, telling the gate guard I had a package to deliver. He waved me inside.

Appleton was still on location in Oregon. His thin-lipped secretary told me she wasn't allowed to give out any personal information on the stars. So I lied. I told her Appleton had *asked* me to see Alex DeMarco as part of the investigation he had hired me to conduct. So, very reluctantly, she gave me DeMarco's address and phone number.

Score one for Kincaid.

I went to a nearby pay phone and punched in the number. Got a servant on the line. Asked to speak to Mr. DeMarco. I told him Lucas Appleton was calling. It worked.

"Lucas?" The same deep-velvet movie voice.

"This is David Kincaid," I said. "I work for Mr. Appleton. I'd like to see you as soon as it's convenient, Mr. DeMarco."

"What about?"

"A personal matter. Something I'd rather not get into over the phone. But I could drive over this afternoon."

"Uh...very well. You have my address?"

"Of course...on Glendower Avenue."

"Then I'll expect you at three," he said. "Sharp."

15

They call DeMarco's place "The House of Horrors," befitting its owner's dark profession, but until I got inside I didn't fully appreciate the name.

Twenty-three hundred Glendower is in the Hollywood Hills, above Griffith Park, and I traveled around a lot of tight, winding curves to reach it. The actor was waiting for me at the gate of his house, holding the leash of a fierce-looking black Doberman who obviously didn't like strangers. The dog was showing me his fangs and growling murderously.

"I have to meet all of my guests personally," said DeMarco. "Otherwise, Bruno considers them intruders. If you were to get inside the gate without me, it's likely he'd tear your throat out."

"I wouldn't like that," I said.

"With Bruno, I don't need a gate-alarm system." And he patted the dog's head. He smiled faintly, then sent Bruno away with a sharp command. We entered the House of Horrors.

It was creepy, to say the least. Floor-to-ceiling oil paintings of Count Dracula, the Wolfman, and Frankenstein. Horror masks pegged to the walls. Rows of signed photos of Boris Karloff, Lon Chaney, Bela Lugosi, Vincent Price, and Barbara Steele. Framed posters celebrating some two dozen fear flicks starring DeMarco.

And a life-sized replica of King Kong's head in the middle of the living room.

The room was dim, with heavy amethyst-colored brocade drapes swagged across the windows.

"I find that sunlight fades the colors," DeMarco said, indicating his paintings and posters. "Please, be seated, Mr. Kincaid. May I offer you something to drink? I often have a brandy in the afternoon."

"Maybe a soft drink," I said. "Anything you've got is fine."

DeMarco snapped his fingers and a tall cadaver of a man instantly appeared at his shoulder. Dressed in black, with a close-shaven head and a blunt, unsmiling face, he seemed to blend in perfectly with the outré surroundings.

"My usual—and a root beer for the gentleman," DeMarco

ordered. The skeletal figure nodded tightly, then drifted back into the shadows.

DeMarco was wearing a blood-red silk dressing gown trimmed in black. Matching slippers covered his feet. His face was as relaxed and as friendly as a vulpine face like his can ever get. The eyes were, of course, dark and penetrating.

"Now...what brings you to the house of DeMarco?" he asked, settling back into a rich assortment of emerald and sapphire-colored tasseled-silk pillows.

"Mr. Appleton has hired me to find a young woman named Justina Phillips," I told him. "I thought you might know her."

He smiled. "And what leads you to such a conclusion?"

I reached into my leather briefcase. "This photo." I handed the color blowup to him.

"Ah...and is this the young lady?"

"Yes. It was taken in 1983, on her tenth birthday."

He looked at me. "And since I seem to be hovering in the background of the picture, you assume that I know her?"

"*Do* you?"

"Unhappily for your search, the answer is no." He handed the print back to me just as our drinks were wheeled in on a french baroque tea cart. The genuine item. Definitely not a reproduction. My root beer looked a little silly sitting in its glass of gilded crystal.

"I don't understand," I told him.

"How could I be in the picture?" He inhaled the fragrance of the brandy, turning the antique snifter slowly in his right hand. "The explanation is quite simple, Mr. Kincaid. In 1983, I was in San Diego making a film. On that particular day we were shooting a sequence in Balboa Park. As I recall, it had to do with my roaming through the trees as a werewolf...or some such nonsense. Thus, the young lady's birthday had nothing to do with me. I obviously glanced in the direction of the party when the photo was taken. Pure happenstance."

"Then you don't know anything about Justina Phillips?"

"Indeed, I do not." He sampled the brandy.

I took a swig of my root beer.

"Justina is a big fan of yours," I told him. "She's watched videos of your films over and over."

He nodded. "I have many dedicated fans, for which I am most grateful. They allow me to maintain my rather self-indulgent lifestyle."

"I just thought there might be a connection..."

DeMarco stood up, putting his brandy glass on the cart. "If you will excuse me, I have some personal matters that need attending." He smiled. "We *have* concluded our little conversation, have we not?"

"Yes...we have." I stood to shake his hand. The flesh was cold, almost clammy. "I thank you for your time, Mr. DeMarco."

"Not a problem. Edward will see you to the gate."

Now the man in black was at *my* shoulder.

He walked me to the front gate without uttering a word.

Spooky. Definitely spooky.

16

What Lyle Anmar had said about the cycle gang stuck in my mind: that the Henchmen were into the very sick business of selling underage females. Not that it was any big surprise. Dope and prostitution provide a solid income for many outlaw cycle gangs across the country.

It was time, however, to find out more about the Henchmen, since it was possible they were tied into Justina's disappearance. A long shot, but possible.

So after I left DeMarco's place I drove out to the beach, to the Malibu Sheriff's Station to see my buddy, Mike Lucero.

Mike is hard-headed, with an abiding contempt for the paranormal, having termed it (on several occasions) "wacko stuff." When I'd tell him about raising my vibrational energy by using the natural psychic power vortex surrounding Sedona, Arizona—or conducting seminars in Pasadena on out-of-body experiences—he'd shake his head. "Why don't you go find a *real* job? I hate to see a friend of mine involved in all this crap."

Yet we *were* friends, and the world he outwardly scoffed at had formed the basis of our friendship. I'd used my special knowledge to help him on a variety of cases—including referring him to psychics who supplied him with what turned out to be vital information in the solution of several homicides. He stills kids me about my "oddball" life, but his mind is opening. Not *much*, admittedly, but Mike's a very stubborn guy.

The truth is, I think he believes a lot more than he's willing to admit about the world of the paranormal. He told me once that his parents were convinced that if you took a long tail hair from a horse and put it in a pail of water, it would turn into a snake within two weeks. Claimed they'd seen it happen with their own eyes.

Mike's office in the Malibu Station is cluttered and musty. When I walked in he met me at the door with a bear hug. He's an emotional guy, and for people he really cares about he doesn't mind showing open affection. Big and tough and tender, that's Mike.

As usual, he couldn't resist a verbal jab at my profession: "Talked to any little green men from Mars lately?"

"I've told you, there *are* no green men—or women—on the planet Mars."

"Yeah, you did at that." He grinned at me. "How the hell you been, Davey?"

No one else calls me Davey. I hate that name. But I let Mike get away with it. All part of our quirky friendship.

"I'm fine," I told him. "You still having trouble with your prostate?"

"Jeez, I *never* should have told you about that," he groaned.

"If you'd just do what I told you..."

"I know, I know. Gobble a handful of fresh pumpkin seeds every day and no more prostate trouble."

"It works," I said. "It really does."

He sat down at his battered oak desk. "How come you're here in the middle of the afternoon? You need some cop help, huh?"

"See," I said brightly, "I told you, you *are* psychic!"

He grinned at that. "So what can I do for you, chum?"

"You can give me some info on the Devil's Henchmen."

"They run out of the north Valley...Sylmar. Not my beat."

"But you can punch up their stat file. Basic data. That's all I'm asking for."

He did that. The data on the computer screen confirmed what Lyle Anmar told me. They were into a variety of unsavory activities. Several of the gang had prison records connected with drugs, prostitution, armed robbery, and criminal assault. Their current leader was a mean piece of business named Bill "Grinder" Mead. Early twenties, spiked hair, big-boned, with muscles to match. He had a long record of his own, but had served only minimal jail time. Obviously, he was a sharp operator.

"Talked to an ex-Henchmen," I told Mike. "He said the gang was supplying out-of-town runaways to local pimps."

Mike shrugged. "So what else is new?"

"There's no way of stopping them?"

"Sure there is," he said. "Sometimes a cop gets lucky. Catches 'em with the pimp and the girls as the deal's going down. But that doesn't happen often. And even when it does, sticking a few scumballs in the slammer doesn't put a dent in anything. Life goes right on. Like with the drugs and the robberies. That's what keeps the gang in pocket money. They take the risk because they know the odds are always on their side." He leaned back in his cracked leather chair, sadness clouding his face. "It's a losing battle, but we cops have to keep up the fight. If we didn't, if we weren't around to hassle these creeps, things would be a hell of a lot worse than they already are."

I thanked him for his help with the Henchmen file, and we talked about getting together for dinner at my place, me and Kelly and Mike and his wife, Carla. A good lady.

"Soon," I promised. "We'll do it soon."

"Okay, Davey, I'm holding you to that. Even Carla can't cook posole the way you can."

He gave me another bear hug and I was out of there.

17

I decided it was time to pay a personal visit to the Henchmen. Not that I had any solid reason; I was just following a gut hunch that told me this was the thing to do, that the Henchmen were somehow related to my bizarre search for Justina Phillips.

Thanks to Mike Lucero, I was registered as an official Sheriff's Consultant, and Mike had helped me obtain a police permit for the snub-nose Smith & Wesson .38 Special I took along that night. Just in case. I was no gunfighter. Despite a fair amount of practice, I was just barely adequate when it came to hitting the vital areas on a target. I hoped I wouldn't have to shoot anybody.

According to what I'd found out from Lucero, the

Henchmen favored a particular Valley hangout—a bar on Sepulveda, near the old San Fernando Mission.

I took the 405 North and parked on the boulevard, directly in front of Bernie's Joint. That was the name of the bar, outlined in a dust-caked scrawl of blinking red neon above the entrance. This was definitely a Triple-B establishment: booze, broads, and bikers. I counted at least a dozen motorcycles, waxed and gleaming, lined up alongside the building, so I figured that most of the Henchmen were inside. This gang was exclusive. Lucero's computer listed only fifteen current members. Nothing like the massive membership of the Hell's Angels.

I tucked the .38 into a clamshell belt holster, buttoned my jacket, and stepped into Bernie's.

The bar was rank with smoke and beer fumes. It wasn't tough spotting the Henchmen. A cluster of them were ranged on tall stools along the bar, each wearing the distinctive club colors—grimy blue-denim sleeveless vests with a horned red skull stitched on the back above the words DEVIL'S HENCHMEN. They were being entertained by several well-endowed gang-mamas wearing Lycra tank leotards with glossy tights. One of the Henchmen, a muscled gorilla with red hair frizzing his bare arms, ambled over to me. "What you want, dude?" He wore a steel bike chain for a belt.

"I want to see Billy Mead."

He lowered his close-shaven bullet head. "The Grinder's occupied."

Mead was sitting at the far end of the bar, a wide-shouldered giant of a man, guzzling beer and playing feelie with a pair of dyed blonde bimbos.

Ignoring the gorilla, I walked over. "Hi, Billy," I said.

He swung toward me. His face was bloated with drink, and his red-rimmed pig eyes squinted through the smoke haze. His spiked hair was rainbow colored, and a pair of snakes coiled in a purple tattoo on his right hand. "Who in hell are *you*, man?"

"I know Lyle Anmar. He used to ride with you."

"That paper-ass!" Mead wiped a white foam of beer from his wide lips. "What about him?"

"Yeah, I know he split with you boys."

"Couldn't cut it," scowled Mead. "No cajones. What did he tell you about us?"

I slipped past his question. "He had a girl for a while, *this* girl..." I showed him the 8 x 10 glossy. "Her name's Justina Phillips."

His face paled. Obviously, the name had meaning to him. My hunch was right; there *was* a connection.

"I never seen her. How come you have her picture?"

I didn't answer that one, either. "I thought you might know something about her."

"You better walk out of here right now, dude," Billy told me. "While you still got legs, that is." He drew a heavy-bladed hunting knife from his boot. "Or should I just cut you in half?"

"Okay, no sweat. I'll leave." I was suddenly scared and nervous. The tension in the room was as thick as the tobacco smoke.

A voice grated behind me: "Let's give him somethin' to remember us by!"

I swung around to face the red-haired gorilla. He had the bike chain in his hand, spinning it like a rodeo roper.

"Back off, Red," I told him, flicking the .38 free of its holster and aiming it at his beer gut. "I came here for information, not trouble. Since you boys can't help me, I'll leave. I don't want a hassle."

Silence. The Henchmen along the bar were all glaring at me. But they didn't move. A .38 is apt to quiet things down a lot.

I left Bernie's joint as rapidly as possible.

And I didn't start breathing easy again until I was rolling down Sepulveda in the Honda with the wind cool and welcome against my sweating face.

18

By the following morning I was into some disturbing thoughts. Suppose Justina had been one of the girls "sold" by the Henchmen? They could have seen her with Lyle and taken her after the breakup. Was she back on drugs? On the streets? Alive? Dead?

I was dressed and ready to leave the house for another chat with Mike Lucero when the door buzzed.

I opened it. The last person I expected to see was outside my front door, standing there in the sunlight. She said, "Hi. I hear you've been looking for me."

It was Justina.

She was staring at me with those dark, intense eyes. "Aren't you going to say anything?"

"Uh...sure, sure. Come in. I'm just...surprised."

"You didn't figure on my coming here, huh?"

"No...I didn't. Where did you get my address?"

"From Bobbi. She said you'd been looking for me, and she had one of your cards. So I came on over. Hope you don't mind."

"No, no. I'm just happy to see you're okay."

We sat down in the living room. Both of us a little nervous. I'd spent so much time and emotion trying to locate the girl who sat facing me that the situation seemed more dream than reality.

Justina was wearing a striped black-and-white tank top, red shorts, and high white heels. Her ears sported large red enamel earrings, and there were red plastic bracelets on both wrists. Her oval face was pale. No lipstick. Which made her dark eyes even more striking. "Are you a detective?" she asked me.

"No," I said. "I'm just a hired hand. I was paid to find you."

"By who?"

"Lucas Appleton. He's a movie producer over at Murdock Studios in Burbank."

"What's he want with me?"

"He saw you playing a bit part...in that earthquake thing you did."

"So?"

"So he thinks you have 'major potential.' Wants to sign you up for his next film. He says he can build you into a star."

Her face twisted in disdain. "Me? A *star*? That's a load of crap."

"I'm no judge of who looks good in front of a camera," I told her. "But Lucas Appleton knows—"

"Knows what?" she cut in. "Does he know *me*? He just wasted his money sending you after me."

"Then...you don't want the chance at a career?"

She lowered her head in defeat. "A career? I just want to *survive*. I'm so screwed-up that just getting through another day takes everything I've got. I can't hold down any kind of job right now—let alone trying to be an actress." Her eyes were agonized. "I'm being torn apart inside." She shook her head. "But you don't know what I'm saying. No way you could."

"Are you doing drugs again? Is that it?"

She pushed a strand of dark hair back from her face with a nervous hand. "No, it's not drugs. It's other things..."

I leaned toward her, meeting her eyes. "Want to talk about it? I'm a good listener."

"Why should I talk to you?"

"Why not? I've invested a lot of time and trouble in trying to find you. Don't you think you could at least tell me *why* you've been running away—and just what you're running from?"

Justina got up, walked to the window, staring out into the morning brightness. Then she wheeled to face me, lips trembling, tears in her eyes. "I don't *know* what I'm running from," she said in a wavering voice. "When the dreams began, I ignored them at first. Then they kept getting worse, turning into nightmares. I used drugs to try and escape them, but that didn't work. So I stopped. With some help. Then I drank for awhile...stayed drunk for a week...but that didn't help, either. The dreams just keep getting worse. More and more...real."

She walked over to my studio couch and sat down limply, biting her lower lip to keep back the tears.

I sat down next to her, taking her hand. She seemed so young and vulnerable, a defeated child lost in the forests of nightmare. "I really want to help," I said.

She nodded. "I believe you, but...I don't know why you'd care about what happens to me."

"Maybe because I don't like to see anyone hurting as badly as you are. In the last few days I've done a lot of thinking about you, Justina. I'm trying to understand you."

"You want to know about the dreams?"

I nodded. "Maybe if you tell me about them, they'll seem less real. I saw Lyle Anmar and he mentioned them. Said they dealt with the supernatural. With demons."

"Just one demon," she said. "It doesn't have a name...or if it does, I don't know what it is. This...this thing...keeps getting stronger. In the early dreams it was in the background—but in each new dream it's getting closer, becoming more real... more *horrible*."

"Does it threaten you?"

"Not exactly. It's like...it wants to...change me."

"Change you how?"

"I don't know. But it seems to have a *purpose*."

She scrubbed at her tear-streaked eyes. "Now, even in the daytime when I'm not dreaming, I can see its face. Grinning at me—as if it knows some special secret."

"This might be an aftereffect of the drugs you took. Sometimes drugs can make dreams seem very real."

She shook her head vigorously. "It was there *before* the drugs. I *told* you..."

"You need help," I said. "And I'm not the one who can help you. I know a clinic where you can receive proper treatment."

Justina pulled back from me so abruptly that one of her earrings popped loose, landing on the couch. She ignored it, staring at me with eyes gone suddenly cold. "You don't *really* want to help me," she snapped. "You just want to put me away somewhere like a crazy person. Well, I'm *not* crazy!" She stood up, still glaring at me.

"I never said that. I was only—"

"Go to Hell, Kincaid!"

She ran from the room and was out of the house before I could reach the door to stop her.

Gone.

Back into hiding.

From the demon inside.

19

Another night. Another victim...

The sour taste of vomit was in her throat and her eyes were red and swollen; her naked skin was bleeding from a dozen abrasions. She knew she would die very soon now, her flesh slashed and savaged, her body ripped asunder by daggered teeth.

She was barely sixteen, yet these were the final moments of her life. What a fool she'd been to run away, to leave Ohio, her home, her parents, her younger brother and sister, to come here to California, to run into a death more horrific than she could ever have imagined.

She retched again in dry heaves that tore at her raw throat. Then she sprawled forward, her face against the slimed stones of her cell. Saliva dribbled from her caked, broken lips.

Why me? The question roared in her mind, spinning in endless circles within her brain.

Why me?

Dear God, why me?

Why?

Why?

20

Lucas Appleton had returned from his location shoot in Oregon when I walked into his office. He smiled at me around one of his unlit cigars. "How are you David?"

Not that he cared, but I said that I was fine.

"The picture's going great," he declared. (That accounted for the smile.) "We're a week ahead of schedule and half a million under budget. Me and the director, we see eye to eye on this baby all down the line. Last director I used was a fag sonuvabitch." He sat down behind his white desk. "Okay—to business. Have you been able to trace the Phillips girl?"

"She traced me," I said, thinking what an offensive toad Appleton really was. The more he shot off his foul mouth, the less I could stomach him. It was good not to be working for him anymore.

He frowned at me. "What do you mean, she traced *you*?"

"Showed up at my house this morning. I told her all about your job offer. She declined."

He leaned across the desk. "Where is she now? I *need* to know."

"What difference does it make where she is?" I said. "She doesn't want to make your movies. Period." I put a slip of paper on his desk: my personal check for four grand.

He picked it up, stared at it numbly.

"The other thousand I'm keeping for my time and expenses," I told him.

"I don't care about the damn money!" The producer was red in the face; a muscle jumped along his jaw line. "Kincaid, I *demand* that you tell me where the Phillips girl can be found."

I said to him what Justina had said to me before she left; I told him to go to Hell.

And headed for my CRX.

21

I had dinner again that night with Kelly. She'd just sold a major essay to *Enquire* disputing the *auteur* theory in American cinema and was in a bubbly mood. When I told her about seeing Justina and about my subsequent meeting with Appleton, she seemed as relieved as I was that the job was over. Ultimately, Kelly declared, the girl must deal with whatever personal demons (or demon) pursued her.

I was very quiet throughout our dinner together, feeling guilty about not being able to help Justina. And I couldn't do anything about it now because I didn't know where she'd gone or how to reach her. She'd vanished again, like a puff of smoke, into the immense hive-swarm of Greater Los Angeles.

Also, I know she didn't *want* my help.

But that didn't change how I felt about her. I couldn't get Justina Phillips out of my mind; her dark eyes continued to haunt me.

I apologized to Kelly for being such a lousy dinner companion and begged off for the rest of the evening, telling her I had to get back on target with my own career. I was going home to prep notes on a seminar I was due to conduct the following month in Palm Springs.

"Would I want to go?"

"Up to you," I said. "Subject is 'The Third Eye: Seeing Beyond the Obvious.'"

"I'll pass. I've already read most of your papers on the Third Eye."

Kelly understood about cutting our date short; she was actually very sweet about it.

I was the moody one.

22

It was after midnight and a wind from the ocean was rattling the pine trees outside the house. I was working in my den on the seminar, trying to focus on my notes, when a sound from the rear of the house caught my attention.

The wind? I didn't think so. This had been a loud, thumping sound. As if the kitchen door was being forced.

I got up quickly, leaving the den and heading for the kitchen. When I reached it saw the dim form of a man directly outside the window. He began smashing at the glass with a wooden baseball bat.

I'd left the .38 in the Honda's glove compartment, and it was the only gun I owned, so I reached for the kitchen knife just as the intruder leaped through the shattered window.

He was on top of me before I had a chance to use the knife. We slammed to the floor together in a writhing tangle of arms and legs, the kitchen knife spinning away from me on the polished linoleum.

He was a big guy in a black-knit ski mask, strong as a sumo wrestler. My eyes bugged as he locked a meaty arm around my neck and started squeezing. Red sparks began dancing inside my head and I knew I had to act fast before the killing pressure got to me. I drove my left elbow back into his groin with enough force to elicit a heavy grunt of pain. That broke the chokehold, and I rolled free, managing to scoop up the fallen kitchen knife.

I lunged for him, blade extended, but he smashed my left kneecap with the wooden bat and I dropped the knife again, clutching at my leg. Now he loomed over me, eyes glittering through the holes in the ski mask. "Where is she?"

"Who?" I gasped, holding my knee. "Where's who?"

"The Phillips girl. Lucas said you saw her yesterday. "Where *is* she?"

"I don't know," I told him. "You can beat the crap out of me, but it won't change the fact that I don't know where she is."

"We'll see if you're telling the truth," he said, ramming the bat into my stomach. It took me a while to get back enough breath to say, "I don't know. Dammit, man, *I don't know.*"

He swung the heavy bat toward my head. I could see it arcing down at me, could even see the grain of the wood, as if everything moved in slow motion. Then it exploded against my skull and a yellow plume of fire roared across my brain.

23

I opened my eyes. Mike Lucero was patting my bleeding scalp with a wet bath towel. I was on the studio couch; obviously, he'd carried me there.

"Hi, pal," I said shakily. "What brings you over? It's pretty late for a social call."

"Somebody spotted a guy riding hell-bent away from here on a red Harley," Mike told me. "Looked suspicious, so he phoned the sheriff's station. Since it was your address, I figured I'd come check on you."

"Glad you did," I said. "But since when are you working nights?"

"Since we got backed up on cases," he said. "I came in tonight to help out."

"So...Doctor Lucero, am I still alive?"

"You look like a Mack truck rolled over you," he growled. "I'm calling an ambulance."

"Oh no, you're not." I sat up, holding the towel against my head. "We're going after the bastard that did this."

"You know who he is? You see his face?"

"No, he was wearing a ski mask. But I recognized his voice and I saw the snake tattoo on his right hand. It was Billy Mead."

"The Grinder!" Mike shook his head. "Why would Mead attack you?"

"He wanted to find somebody I've been looking for. A girl. Figured I knew where she was."

"Do you?"

"No, and that's what I told him. But he didn't seem to believe me." I stood up gingerly, testing my left leg. The knee throbbed painfully, but I could walk. I put aside the towel; my head had stopped bleeding. "I'll tell you the full story on the way to get Mead."

"I'd better call for backup."

"No, Mike, it's just you and me on this one. I don't want any cops around when I get my hands on him."

"What about *me*? *I'm* a cop."

"You're my friend. There's a difference."

"I'd have to be completely out of my gourd to go out against the Henchmen with a smashed-up spook hunter in the middle of the frigging night."

But that's exactly what he did.

24

We took Mike's police cruiser. Our first stop was Bernie's Joint on Sepulveda. When we walked in, we found several Henchmen at the bar. Mead wasn't among them. The bikers glared at us sullenly, poised for action, until Mike flashed his badge. Then they backed off fast. Cop trouble was the last thing they wanted.

It turned out that the bartender knew Billy's home address and with a little persuasion (Mike threatened to rip off his head), he gave it to us.

We drove over there. To a seedy apartment building just two miles from Bernie's. Mead was on the second floor, number 212, and Mike didn't bother to announce us. He just put his shoulder into that flimsy wooden door and smashed through, gun in hand. I was right behind him with my .38 Special out and ready.

We heard a female shriek from the inner bedroom; a well-rounded blonde in a black net bra and tight red hot pants ran past us in the hall. She took off down the stairs while we headed for the bedroom.

Bill was in there, sitting cross-legged on the mattress, buck naked. He had a sawed-off leveled at us.

"Put down that shotgun," Mike ordered, his .45 aimed at Mead's hairy chest. "I'm with the Sheriff's Department, and you're under arrest."

"For what?" Billy demanded.

Of course he recognized me, and he knew damn well why we were there. But he was a mean piece of goods and his grip on the sawed-off didn't waver.

My throat was dry. If Mead triggered that shotgun we'd be perforated dog meat.

Mike didn't seem shaken by those twin barrels staring at us. His .45 was no match for a sawed-off at his range, but Lucero backs down to nobody.

"I told you," he said coldly, spacing his words: "Put... down...that...weapon!" He let the barrel of the automatic drop an inch. "Or do you want me to blow your nuts off?"

"You got nothin' on me," whined Mead. "An' you got no call to come bust-assin' in here with guns. I got my rights!"

"You gave those up when you came at me tonight with a baseball bat," I said, my .38 pointed at him. I was gripping it so hard my fingers ached.

"How do you know it was me?"

"The tattoo on your right hand," I said.

"I'll tell you just one more time, punk," rasped Mike. "Either you put down that weapon or —"

He didn't get a chance to finish the threat. Billy did a wild roll off the mattress, firing as he hit the floor.

The rolling action threw off his aim and the double barrel shotgun charge took out the top half of the bedroom door, but it didn't touch Mike or me.

Lucero triggered his automatic. Twice. Both rounds socked home in Mead's body. The first skidded across his ribs, but the second got him square in the chest.

He dropped the shotgun, clawing at his bleeding upper body, eyes rolled white with shock.

Mike holstered the .45 and stood over Mead. His voice was level now, the hardness gone. "I'm sorry you made me do that, Billy," he said. "Real sorry."

"That makes...two of us," gasped Mead. Blood bubbles

were already breaking at his lips; he didn't have long.

"Got a phone here?" Mike asked.

Billy shook his head.

"Stay with him," Mike told me. "I'm going out to the car and call for an ambulance."

I nodded—and Mike quickly exited the bedroom. Billy was trying to tell me something. I knelt down next to him, leaning in close to hear the words.

"It...wasn't *me*...I was...sent."

"Who sent you?"

"Wanted...her...Justina...real bad...for...one of his girls."

"Are you talking about a pimp?"

A faint shake of his head. "These girls...they were...*special*." He coughed raggedly, red froth at his mouth. "Just...one a month...young, pretty ones...he pays high..."

"Who? Who's been paying you for the special girls?"

Billy tried to form more words, but couldn't. Blood ran steadily down his chin. He was fading fast. I could hear sirens in the distance as Mike returned to the room.

"He gonna make it?"

In answer, the biker's head fell back. Mead's body twitched once, a spastic death twitch—and then he was gone.

Maybe he'd learned enough this time around so his next life wouldn't be so lousy. I hoped so.

Mike looked at me. His eyes were troubled. We didn't say anything as the sirens got louder.

25

I decided not to tell Lucero what Billy had said about the "special girls." It was something I wanted to deal with on my own.

Took me a long time that night to get to sleep; I had a lot

of anger inside me.

When Lucas Appleton showed up at his studio office at ten-thirty the next morning, I was there waiting for him. I'd gotten rid of his thin-lipped secretary a half-hour earlier, telling her that the producer had a head cold and wouldn't be coming in. She was to drive over to his house for some emergency dictation. I didn't want her around for my little talk with Appleton.

When he walked in I was sitting in his cream-colored leather desk chair. He looked surprised to see me—as well as annoyed because I was in his chair. I stood up, walking around the desk to face him.

"I'm here because of Billy," I said. My tone was edged.

Appleton lifted an eyebrow. "Billy? I don't know anyone name Billy."

"Not anymore you don't. Billy's dead. And in case you're wondering, he didn't get a thing out of me last night when you sent him to my place."

"Look Kincaid, I don't know what the hell you're talking about."

"Oh, I think you do," I said, grabbing him by the front of his shirt and slamming him hard against the office wall. "I think you know *exactly*—"

"How dare you manhandle me!" he sputtered.

"You're lucky I'm not taking a baseball bat to your head! That's what your biker boy did to me."

I shoved him backwards onto the couch and he landed with a thump solid enough to dislodge his mirrored shades.

His eyes were wide and frightened; I was getting to him.

"Billy Mead used your name when he broke into my place last night," I told him. "His exact words were: 'Lucas said you saw her yesterday.' Meaning Justina. Obviously, you sent him to beat her address out of me."

"That's insane!"

"There's more. Before he died, Mead told me he's been supplying 'special' girls to someone who's paying a high price for them—and that this buyer wanted Justina Phillips 'real bad,' as he put it." I stood above Appleton, hands fisted. "*You're* the buyer. Everything fits. You never intended to *hire* Justina, you wanted her for the same perverted reason you wanted these other girls."

"Get out of my office!" The producer's face was puffed and livid. "You can't come in here and accuse me of such nonsense! I don't buy women!"

I was about to go for him again when two big security guards, alerted by the racket, grabbed me, painfully twisting my arms behind my back.

"You want this creep arrested, Mr. Appleton?"

"Uh...no." Appleton looked badly shaken. "Just...have him kept off the lot. He's mentally unbalanced. Now get him out of here."

They did that, fast-walking me to my Honda and making sure I exited Murdock Studios.

I knew why Appleton hadn't pressed charges against me. He was afraid I'd tell the cops what I told him. But I couldn't. Not yet. Because I had no proof that he was the buyer. I was certain in my gut that he was the one, and by facing him at the studio I'd hoped to force an admission out of him. But that hadn't worked.

There was one key question that I kept asking myself, over and over: was Lucas Appleton buying these girls for himself—or for someone else?

26

I felt I *had* to find Justina—that a demonic force was closing in on her and that I might, somehow, be able to avert its course.

The weather reflected my mood; the day had suddenly darkened. Heavy clouds from the Mexican tropics had rolled in like a host of towering, bloated figures in soot-black clothing. A rainstorm was brewing, unseasonable for August in L.A. Usually we don't get rain in the summer.

I returned home to a message from Kelly on my answering machine. She was off to Paris, on assignment for a fashion magazine, and would see me when she got back.

An hour later, under a shrouded sky, I was on the freeway, headed for downtown, carrying in my coat pocket what I hoped would provide a lead to Justina.

I was relieved to find Irene Hopwood at home. When I rang the bell from the porch of her big Victorian house, I saw her image rippling through the stained-glass front window as she answered the door. She opened the screen, giving me a warm smile.

"I tried to call you first," I told her, "but you were out. I took a chance anyhow and came on down here."

"I just got home," she said. "Been shopping all afternoon. If you've got feet as wide as mine, finding the right shoes can be a real hassle. Maybe if I were a better psychic I could visualize them and know just where to look."

"May I talk to you?" I asked.

"Of course, David." She gestured me in. "You know you're always welcome. But I'm afraid I didn't buy any of those chocolate chip cookies you like so much."

I grinned. "I'll manage to survive without 'em."

We sat down on two smoked-orange velour chairs in her parlor. The day's gloom was aborted by a pair of tall, heavily-scrolled Victorian bronze lamps. They cast a warm yellow radiance over the room.

"At least I can offer you tea," Irene said.

"No, thanks. I just came to show you this." I took Justina's red earring from my coat pocket. It glittered in the lamplight.

"Belongs to the young woman I talked to you about last time. Justina Phillips. She left it at my place."

"Then you *did* find her?"

"No, she came to me. And then promptly disappeared again. I was hoping the earring might help me locate her."

Irene's face was somber. "I'm sorry to hear you're still involved with her. I warned you that by searching for this individual you were moving into a very dangerous area—toward a destructive force of darkness."

"I remember," I said. "And, believe me, I don't discount your warning—but I feel that she *needs* me, that somehow I must reach her before she's destroyed."

"And what if *you're* destroyed with her?"

"That's a chance I'm willing to take. I don't have all the answers, Irene. And I don't *know* what I'll be going up against. But I have to try."

Irene looked at me steadily, concern in her shaded gray eyes. "In her mother's photo, I sensed great evil. Perhaps the two have now united."

"That's possible," I admitted.

"Then you still want me to 'read' the earring?"

"I do. She was wearing it when she came to see me, so it should carry strong vibrations."

I handed the enameled red earring to Irene. She accepted it hesitantly, as if it might burn her flesh. "We're dealing here with demonic powers. Are you *certain* you want me to proceed?"

I nodded. "I'm certain."

She pressed both hands firmly around the object, leaning forward, picking up the earring's vibrations as they began to resonate within her own force field.

She closed her eyes. A ripple of movement shook her body and her breathing deepened. "This person is...is..."

"Yes? What do you see?"

"Darkness. There is a terrible darkness surrounding her. It's...palpable. A *physical* presence. There's a name...*Sargoth*." Abruptly, she opened her eyes. "This is very bad, David. Dangerous. I don't like what I'm getting."

I didn't tell her who Sargoth was; that would have disturbed her even more. "Do you sense danger for Justina?"

"I don't know. The negative vibrations—I can't separate them. The darkness is overwhelming."

"I need to find her as soon as possible," I said. "Try and give me a location."

She pressed the earring to her forehead and closed her eyes again. "A beach. A house...facing the ocean. White. The house is painted white."

"But where is it? We've got a helluva long coastline!"

"It's here...in this area. Southern California. The Los Angeles area. She...she's with a friend. A female."

Maybe Justina was back with Bobbi Graham in Venice. But that building didn't face the ocean—and it wasn't white.

Irene told me she could get no more and seemed anxious to return the earring to me. Like ridding herself of a poisonous snake.

When I left Irene Hopwood I was frightened. I told myself to give it up, to stop searching for Justina, to allow her to work out her own destiny. I knew I was entering an area of serious personal risk, possibly beyond my limits. When you're in a boat and spot a whirlpool churning the water ahead of you, the last thing you do is row toward it. You pull back to keep from being sucked under. That's how I felt—that if I kept up this senseless quest I'd be sucked under, whirled into darkness.

By the time I reached my Honda a hard rain had begun, sizzling on the pavement like grease in a skillet. The sky was ominous and sullen, and the late afternoon sun had retreated behind thickly-massed clouds. It was smart to get out of a storm's way.

I wasn't.

27

Back home I did some basic research in my library. (Of which I am immodestly proud. Over 25,000 well-chosen volumes I began collecting when I was ten, most of them relating to the paranormal and supernatural.) Sargoth was listed in *A History of Demonology* as the progenitor of a ghoulish brood of shape-change demons dating back to Neolithic times. They were said to have a strong taste for human flesh. Such a creature was known as a "broxa."

Could it be possible that Justina's mother was one of these? A lineal descendant of Sargoth, the Father of Demons? Was *she* the demonic presence that haunted Justina's dreams?

"Kincaid," I said aloud, firmly shutting the book, "I think you're round the bend on this one."

It wasn't that I didn't have a healthy respect for the supernatural; I believe that there are many forces in this bizarre, wonderful universe of ours which exist on planes beyond the rational. But I had personally never encountered a demon, anymore than I'd seen a flying saucer. Still...I ripped a page from the book, folding it into my pocket.

I decided to quit thinking about broxas and check out my idea that Justina might once again be living with Bobbi Graham. Maybe they'd moved to a new location facing the ocean.

"She'd never move back with me," Bobbi declared when I reached her on the phone. "Our life styles are too spaced out. There's no way we could cut it together anymore."

"Okay," I said. "You've got my home number. Contact me if you hear from her."

With my next call I struck pay dirt. Lyle Anmar knew about a friend of Justina's who had a house right on the beach in Trancas.

"Her name is Linda Galvin," he told me. "She's a commercial artist. Paints stuff for all the major greeting card companies."

"What's she like?"

"Ash blonde. Good looker. In fact, she'd be a real knockout except for the pink scar along the right side of her face. Said she got it when she was a kid—in a car accident."

"Could Justina be living with her?"

"Maybe. They're close pals. But, like I told you, I've been totally out of touch."

I thanked Anmar, telling him that he'd been a big help.

The phone book provided me with Linda Galvin's address.

I drove there.

The darkness was closing in.

28

As I swung the CRX onto Pacific Coast Highway, the storm was in full force. Rain smashed down from a charcoal sky.

Trancas is an upscale community a few miles north of Malibu. Several well-known film personalities have homes in the area. Steve McQueen used to live there when he was married to Ali MacGraw. Obviously, Linda Galvin was doing just fine with her art. Losers don't live in Trancas.

Her house was typical. Long, low, rambling—an ultra-modern stone-and-glass job built right on the sand, with a wide porch facing the ocean.

And it was white.

I came in from the beach side. Thunder rumbled overhead

like a cannon and the sea was in turmoil, sending in its battalions of wind-crested waves like troops charging an enemy shore.

The steps leading up to Galvin's porch were slick with rain and blown sand. I tapped on the sliding glass door and waited, getting out my Sheriff's Consultant ID. Nobody answered. The house was totally dark inside. I tapped again, louder this time. Still no reply.

I leaned close to the cold glass, trying to peer in, but I couldn't make out anything. The interior was as black as the dark side of the moon.

I tried the sliding glass door. It was unlocked. Which bothered me. People in Trancas don't go away leaving their houses open.

Something was wrong inside.

Should I go back to my Honda for my .38? Or should I phone Mike Lucero? But what would I tell him? I wasn't even sure that Justina was living here. That was a guess, based on what Lyle Anmar had told me.

I slid the glass door open. It whispered smoothly back along oiled runners and I stepped inside. Immediately, I recognized a strong, overwhelming odor. Newly-spilled blood. I groped my way to a table lamp and snapped it on.

Blood was everywhere. Spattered on walls, smeared across furniture, streaked along wood flooring. Someone had been butchered in this room like a steer in a slaughterhouse.

Numbly, I snapped on another lamp. This illuminated the killing site—behind a long, sectional sofa. The beige rug was soaked in dark crimson—and *part* of a body was there.

A human arm, ripped violently from the shoulder, was lying near one of the polished oak end tables. The flesh was soft and rounded, and a bracelet still adorned the wrist. The arm of a young female. (*Justina?* Had I arrived too late to save her? Had a monstrous creature from her dreams materialized to destroy her?)

Then I saw that a smeared blood trail led toward the rear of the house. The killer had obviously dragged the body out of the living room and along a short hallway. I followed the gory trail to a closed door at the end of the hall. A bathroom.

Opening the door was one of the most difficult and unnerving acts of my life. It required full willpower to force my hand to turn the knob.

The raw smell of blood and body wastes assaulted my nostrils, overpowering and horrible. I fumbled for the wall switch, activated it. The sudden glare of fluorescent brightness shocked my eyes.

She was in the tub. What was left of her, that is. Much of her body was missing, whole chunks of it, as if a Great White had been at her, slashing and devouring. Gobbets of flesh had plugged the drain and the corpse was literally swimming in blood.

I'd never seen anything like this. I gagged. A sour wave of bile welled up from my stomach, causing me to double over and spew the contents of my last meal over the blood-puddled tile floor.

Most of the head was intact, although it lolled grotesquely sideways, almost bitten through the neck. Ash blonde hair was clotted with blood and I could clearly see the long pink scar along the right side of the face.

The dead girl was Linda Galvin.

I'd been right about Justina; she *had* been living here in Trancas. I found her clothes in one of the closets, including the striped black-and-white tank top she'd worn at my place.

But where is she now?

Walking back toward the living room, I saw that a message had been scrawled in blood on the wall near the hall doorway. Reading it, I knew suddenly, chillingly, where

I'd find Justina.

I had one more thing to do before I left this place of death. I went into the kitchen, opened the fridge, took out a carton of milk. I emptied it into the sink, rinsed it out with cold water, and carried it back into the hall...

29

I called the Malibu Sheriff's Station from an outside phone, with rain threading the sides of the glass half-booth. I asked for Mike Lucero and they told me to call him at home, that he was back on days.

His wife answered, and I asked Carla to put Mike on the line, telling her that it was urgent.

"What's up, Davey?" His voice was solid and reassuring.

"A young woman named Linda Galvin was butchered tonight at her beach house in Trancas," I told him.

There was a pause on the line before Mike spoke. "*Butchered*?"

"That's the only word for it."

"Give me the address." I did that, and he said he'd call it in to the station.

"I need to ask a favor, Mike. A big one."

"So ask."

"I think I know who killed Linda Galvin," I said. "But I need you with me when I check it out. Just the two of us."

"Again?" he groaned. "Hey, Kincaid, you're not Batman and I'm not Robin the Boy Wonder. If you know where the killer is, then we send in cops to deal with the situation."

"I can't be sure I'm right. It's a wild theory based on a lot of stuff you wouldn't understand. But if I *am* right, then cops with guns won't do any good. It's going to take more than bullets to finish this."

"What the hell are you talking about?"

"If I told you what I'm talking about, you'd refuse to help me. Trust me, Mike. I *need* you with me tonight. I don't want to do this alone."

"Do *what?*"

"You'll find out when I see you. Please. Meet me. I'm asking you as a friend."

Despite his better judgement, Lucero met me exactly one hour later in Griffith Park. The storm was still bad, and rain slashed down like bright swords in front of our headlights.

I waved Mike over. He left his car and climbed into my Honda, shaking rain from his hair and glaring at me as I started the engine. "Where are we going?"

"To the House of Horrors," I said.

30

I braked the Honda to a quiet stop at twenty-three hundred Glendower, cutting the lights and engine. The sound of drumming rain intensified and the night darkness moved in, thick and menacing around us.

On the way up the hill I had told Mike what I'd found in Trancas, and why I was convinced that a demon had murdered Linda Galvin.

He stared at me. "Demons don't exist, Davey, and you damn well know it."

"This one does," I said. "Or I should say, *they* do."

"They?"

"There's more than one inside the house. Broxas. Witch-demons. Flesh eaters. Part of a breed dating back to Neolithic times. Very strong—and very dangerous."

I had taken along the page I'd removed from *A History of Demonology*. Now I showed it to Lucero. "This is what we'll be dealing with." The steel engraving portrayed two fanged demons locked in combat.

Mike nodded. "You were right...what you said earlier—that if you'd told me any of this over the phone I'd have refused to meet you tonight."

"But it's true, Mike."

"*It's crap!*"

"Come inside with me and I'll *prove* it. They're in the house, Mike, and we have to kill them."

"Oh yeah?" And he snorted. "And just how do you kill a friggin' demon?"

"I know how. But you've got to help me."

"Whose place is this?"

"It belongs to Alex DeMarco."

"The horror actor?"

"He's more than an actor," I said. "And more than human. He's a broxa."

"You're *serious* about all this, aren't you?"

"It's life or death, Mike. Justina Phillips is in there. I've come for her—and I'm going inside with or without you."

He sighed. "Okay, I'll tag along. To make sure you don't get yourself in trouble with DeMarco. Maybe I can explain to him that you're not really a cat burglar, you're just a nut on the supernatural."

"You'll see I'm telling this straight once we're inside," I said, opening the car door.

I got out, carrying the milk carton and a long three-cell metal flashlight.

"What's with the milk?"

"It's not milk, it's blood. And we're going to need it."

"You're planning to give DeMarco a transfusion?"

I ignored the wisecrack. "There's a dog named Bruno guarding the place. A black Doberman. I can handle him."

I said this as I was picking the gate lock with a thin sliver of steel, a trick I'm very good at.

"We don't even have a search warrant," groaned Lucero. "We're gonna get our ass sued!"

"Stay out here until I take care of the dog," I said. "And keep your gun ready in case you have to shoot him." I stepped through the gate.

"This I gotta see," Mike said.

Right on cue, Bruno came galloping out of the night, black on black, his muscled body shining with rain, teeth bared, snarling savagely.

I devoutly hoped my theory about the creature was right. If it wasn't, Mike would have to put a .45 slug through him to keep him from tearing my throat out. I waited until he was almost on me before I flipped open the carton, whipping it toward him.

A long twine of blood spattered over him and he fell back, howling wildly. Instantly, his body dissolved into the wet night grass.

Mike was bug-eyed. "I don't believe what I just saw," he intoned softly. "That dog...he...he just *melted!*"

"It wasn't really a dog," I told Mike, holding the gate open for him. I didn't have time to explain that Bruno was a familiar, a creature attendant to a witch-demon, who in this case had assumed the form of a dog. The best way to kill one is with the blood of a broxa victim, and Linda's had done the job neatly. "*Vamanos!* We need to act fast if we're going to surprise DeMarco."

And we moved rapidly toward the house.

31

We got lucky. One of the lower-story windows was unlatched and we were able to enter the house without setting off any alarms.

I led Mike along a gloomed hallway toward the library. (I'd passed by it the first time I visited DeMarco.) My .38 was still in the Honda; I'd forgotten to put it in my coat. I hoped I wouldn't need it, that if any gunplay was necessary, Mike's .45 would provide us with ample firepower.

The house was cemetery-quiet. The sound of the outside storm was heavily muted, as if God had turned down the volume.

"You sure DeMarco's at home?"

"Bank on it. I know that Justina is here—and where she is, he'll be."

We entered the library. The room was huge, with a deep stone fireplace. I estimated there were at least five thousand volumes packed into the ceiling-to-floor bookcases which lined the room.

"There's a tunnel in here that leads below," I said. "We just have to find it."

"How do you know about a tunnel?"

"There was an article in *Contemporary Architecture* about the guy who built this place," I told him. "It mentioned a tunnel behind one of the bookcases leading down into the wine cellar. I think that's where they are."

I was checking out each bookcase, trying to locate the right one.

"This is Looney Tunes," Mike said. "I feel like a damn fool."

"Got it!" I said in triumph. A large bookcase near the fireplace swung back to reveal the wide mouth of a tunnel, with steps in cut stone leading downward. It smelled damp and fetid. Below us, a faint glow from the cellar tinted the walls.

"Told you they were down there," I whispered.

"There's a light on all right," Mike admitted. "But we don't know *who's* down there."

I put a finger to my lips. "*Real* quiet," I warned as I entered the tunnel. "And be prepared for anything."

Mike followed me down the curved stone stairs with his .45 out, so I knew he was serious.

The tunnel got brighter as we descended. We could hear sounds now—the horrific sounds of teeth on bone, ripping of flesh...

I knew what they signified. A blood feast was in progress and the victim was undoubtedly one of the homeless young girls picked up by the Henchmen and sold to Appleton, who passed them on to DeMarco as a sexual diversion. Of course, I was sure Appleton had no idea of their actual disposition— that they were used not for sex, but to slake a demon's monstrous hunger. That was Alex DeMarco's little secret.

The tunnel ended—and we now had a clear view of the feast as we pressed into the deep shadows at the edge of the wine cellar.

My sense of revulsion was blunted somewhat because I had known what to expect, and because I had already seen what had been done to Linda Galvin—but Mike was visibly shuddering. His face was ashen and his mouth twisted at the horrors confronting us.

Justina *was* with DeMarco, and when I saw her there, I realized that my quest had been without hope, that I could never have saved her.

The transformation had been completed.

She was in a bestial half-crouch, hunched naked over the newly-slain corpse of a young girl. Her body was covered in gore as she gnawed at a detached leg bone, eyes glittering, her hair matted with blood.

She still maintained human form, as did Alex DeMarco, naked beside her, sharing this celebratory meal with his demonic offspring.

The message on the wall in Trancas, scrawled there in

her victim's blood, had told me where Justina had gone after slaughtering Linda Galvin:

> TONIGHT I HAVE ACHIEVED MY DESTINY
> I KNOW WHO MY REAL MOTHER IS
> I AM GOING TO HER NOW

At last, mother and daughter were united.

Alex DeMarco had been Leona Stoddard...just as, in an earlier era, he had been actress Louise Collins. As a shape-change witch-demon, he was able to transform himself—at will—into a fully-functioning man or woman. As Leona, he had given birth to Justina. But he knew she had to be left alone and allowed to mature gradually. The dreams first, then the reality. DeMarco kept track of her for awhile (the photo at her tenth birthday party), but had lost contact as she grew older. As she neared her final transformation, he wanted her badly. That's why he had Appleton and the Henchmen looking for her. They didn't know *why* DeMarco wanted her. Since they regularly supplied young women, Justina would be just another of many.

But, at full maturation, she had found her true parent. Blood had called to blood, and she *knew*, instinctively, where to go.

To the house of Alex DeMarco.

32

I'd been putting all of this together in my mind, but until I found Linda Galvin's half-devoured corpse it didn't lock into place for me.

Tonight, at this moment, it was all too real.

Back at the Trancas house I'd filled the milk carton with the dead girl's blood, dipping the carton in the tub until it was full. My plan was simple: pour a circle of Linda's blood around the demons, then set it afire. A broxa cannot pass through a circle of victim's blood—and broxas *can* be destroyed by fire.

Now I realized that my plan had an inherent problem: how could I immobilize two demons long enough for me to pour the circle of blood? Finding them down here in the wine cellar, however, solved my problem; there was only one exit—through the tunnel. All I had to do was pour a line of blood across the floor in front of the tunnel and put a match to it. The demons would not be able to cross the line, and they'd burn with the house.

I heard a shout from above. I had entirely forgotten about DeMarco's man, Edward. His cry alerted Justina and DeMarco. Like predatory animals, their heads lifted, eyes probing the cellar, picking us out of the darkness.

"Kill the sonuvabitch!" I yelled at Lucero as Edward rounded the tunnel's final curve and came at us with an upraised ax.

Mike didn't hesitate. He fired directly into Edward's face—and the cadaverous creep dropped the ax as Lucero's bullets took his head apart.

At least *he* was no demon.

Justina and DeMarco were watching us calmly, sure of themselves, figuring there was no way we could escape. They were too fast and deadly.

"Bastards!" screamed Lucero, swinging his gun toward them. The roar of the big .45 was deafening in the walled cellar. But, just as I expected, the heavy rounds were totally ineffective; bullets cannot harm a broxa.

He gaped at them, believing, at last, that I was right, that what he now faced was truly demonic.

They were amused. Their gore-smeared lips pulled back in grotesque smiles. I'd never seen smiles like that.

But I still had my plan...

I pushed Mike toward the stairs, yelling "Blood! Stay back!" I raised the carton—but I wasn't quick enough. They sprang forward like a pair of jungle cats, knocking the carton from my grasp and pulling us away from the tunnel. Mike tried to fight, viciously clubbing at them with the barrel of his gun, but the blows were useless.

We were thrown to the cellar floor. When Mike lunged upward again, DeMarco delivered a crushing blow which knocked him senseless. He lay face down, unmoving. But Mike wasn't dead; I could see him breathing.

DeMarco finally spoke. "Did you really think you could trap us down here, Mr. Kincaid? That is quite impossible. We are far stronger than you might imagine."

Justina leveled her dark eyes on me. "We could easily smash our way out of this cellar without having to cross your line of blood," she said.

DeMarco moved to the nearest concrete wall, lashing out with his right fist. The wall cracked open, a deep fissure splitting the concrete.

"I'm impressed," I said, fighting to maintain emotional stability. Terror was forming at the edge of my mind. I couldn't give in to it; I *had* to keep my wits clear.

"You should never have followed me," Justina said, her voice cold as the grave. "It will cost you your life."

"It's *your* life you should worry about," I said. A new plan was forming. A desperate one.

Her eyes flashed. "What do you mean?"

"Violent death is part of your heritage," I said. "A parent broxa is driven to devour its young once the offspring has reached maturity. Like the black widow spider devours its mate. Why do you think DeMarco wanted to find you so badly? You'll be dead before sunup, torn apart by your own loving parent."

"He lies!" hissed DeMarco. "He's trying to set us against one another so he can escape."

"You're younger and more powerful than he is," I told Justina. "You've just come into your full strength. You can destroy him and avert your fate."

She laughed scornfully. "And why should I believe anything you say of the broxa? You fear us. You know how horrible your death will be at our hands."

"Then consider this," I said, snatching the page with the reproduced steel engraving from the pocket of my coat and tossing it to her. "From *A History of Demonology*. It proves what I've told you."

She stared at the engraved illustration, showing a young broxa being torn apart by its parent demon. The caption verified my words.

DeMarco ripped it from her hand. "Don't listen to him. He seeks to divide us!" He swung his head toward me, eyes blazing. "And shall die for it!"

He pulled me toward him, his mouth wide, head dipping for my throat. His teeth glittered like blood-stained daggers under the cellar lights.

I fought desperately to break free, but his strength was awesome; I was helpless in his grip. The terror in my mind swept up to engulf me. In another second he'd tear my throat out.

Suddenly, DeMarco jerked back, screaming in pain. Attacking behind him, Justina had torn a sizable gobbet of raw flesh from his left shoulder.

He released me, pivoting to clash with his angry offspring. They were snarling at each other, the sounds only half-human.

This was my chance. I closed my fingers around the carton

of blood. It was intact; I hadn't had time to open it again before it had been knocked to the floor.

I edged around the grappling demons as they writhed in slashing battle. I opened the carton and began pouring the blood circle. Completed, it totally surrounded them, a barrier neither could cross.

I got my arms around Mike's chest and dragged him to the stairs. He was groaning, beginning to come around. I pulled a matchbook from my coat. Fumbled to open. Struck a match. Then I seized the fallen book page that DeMarco had discarded and ignited it, creating a small torch in my hand. I flipped it at the edge of the crimson circle.

Blood from a broxa's victim will burn like jet fuel, and the entire area erupted into a sudden flame.

Yet DeMarco and Justina paid no heed to the conflagration. Lost in a death struggle, they had now reverted to their loathsome demon forms, scaly and terrible, locked together, tearing savagely at one another with tooth and claw.

Near the tunnel entrance, Mike had regained full consciousness and staggered to his feet, a hand braced against the wall. "What the hell's going on?"

"Up the stairs!" I yelled at him. The fire was spreading rapidly. "Move!"

We plunged back into the tunnel, coughing and choking from the dense smoke, climbing steadily upward as the fire raged below.

By dawn, despite the best efforts of the L.A. City firefighters, the House of Horrors was totally destroyed. Only black ash and scorched stone remained.

The storm was over and the sun rose into a cloudless summer sky.

The hellish hunt for Justina Phillips had ended.

THREE

THE HORROR
AT WINCHESTER HOUSE

Halloween Night, 1977
Four of the five people seated at a circular oak table in the Blue Room of Winchester House were giggling at the instruction of clasped hands. The four, all Stanford undergrads, were there on a lark. Scott and Justin had challenged Laura and Brooke to participate in a séance in which an attempt would be made to invoke the spirit of Sarah Pardee Winchester, who had died here, at age 82, in 1922. The legendary mistress of Winchester House had been a recluse for decades before her death. Locals had dubbed the old woman a "witch."

When their dates accepted the challenge, Scott and Justin—scions of politically well-connected, financially-powerful San Francisco families, and graduates of the same Eastern prep school—had been granted permission to conduct the midnight séance in the same room in which Sarah was said to have "communed with the spirits" each evening during her adult lifetime.

"This is *dumb*," Laura had declared as they took their places at the circular table. "Who would believe that we're actually trying to contact some old dead woman who's rotting in her grave."

"She finished rotting a long time ago," Scott said. "Only a few yellow bones left now…and maybe her teeth, if she had any left when she kicked off."

"It's a waste of time," Laura responded.

"I think it's cool," said Brooke. "I've always wanted to meet a ghost."

"Bet you won't think it's so cool when the old lady grabs your booty in the dark," teased Justin.

Madame Balchava, the sour-faced Russian medium hired to conduct the séance, glared at the four of them as the lights dimmed in the room. "If, and I say *if*, we are fortunate enough to call Sarah Winchester forth from her sojourn beyond mortality, I can assure you there will be no physical contact. In fact, she will not actually appear before our eyes, but will speak through me. My body will contain hers and I will then be able to act as her conduit."

"It'll be a hoot," said Scott.

Madame gave him a withering look. "I caution all of you to take this séance with utmost seriousness. One does not trifle with the spirits of those who have departed our sphere."

It was dark now, the only illumination a small yellow candle in the exact center of the table.

"Am I then to proceed?" asked the medium.

"Proceed away," said Justin—which is when Madame Balchava instructed them to clasp hands around the table. Giggling, the four young people complied.

"Are you scared?" whispered Scott to Brooke.

She ignored him.

"If we're going to do this, then let's get to it," said Laura.

Madame Balchava responded with irritation. "I demand total silence." She hesitated, calming herself, then resumed her induction, beginning to speak slowly, rhythmically, in a tranquilizing, artificial cadence. "Each of you will clear your thoughts...quiet your bodies...open your minds...and your consciousness...to the presence...of Sarah Pardee Winchester. She must feel welcome among us."

The giggling ceased as Madame Balchava, sitting ramrod-straight in a high-backed chair, began to chant deep in her throat. The light from the single candle shimmered across her closed eyes as the slow chanting grew in volume.

Then with shocking abruptness, the heavy bronze bell in the tower of the Winchester House began to toll.

"Ah..." nodded Madame Balchava. "She rings to acknowledge that she has joined us."

"This is bogus," said Laura.

"*Quiet!*" the medium's voice snapped like a whip. "Contact demands silence." Then: "Enter, Sarah Winchester. My body is yours!"

Her muscles stiffened. Her face began to change configuration as her lips twisted in an ugly grimace and the muscles of her jaw grew taut. She began rocking in her chair. "I feel...her presence," she murmured. "Speak through me, oh spirit...I implore thee...*Speak!*"

The medium's body jerked. Her eyes popped wide, rolled white. A thin spittle coated her lips. Then, in a cracked, quavery voice, she formed words. The tone was angry, tinged with venom. "Why have you defiled my house? Why have you dared to disturb my rest? To mock me? To demonstrate your lamentable ignorance of that which is beyond your ability to comprehend? You disgust me! No longer will I permit this invasion of my home. I herewith invoke the Thirteen to deal with those who dare to enter Winchester House from this night forward." The medium's body continued to twist and writhe.

"Holy crap!" whispered Justin. "This is *real!*"

"After this night, no living creature will be permitted here!" The quavering voice rose on a note of fury. "*Leave my house! Now!*"

The candle abruptly hissed out, plunging the room into cold darkness.

*   *   *

What can I tell you about the occult world? I should have all the answers, right? Just ask me, David Kincaid, intrepid investigator of the paranormal. I know you have questions to ask.

For example: do I believe in ghosts? Well, I've seen them, dealt with them, been frightened by them—and they certainly exist in what I'm about to relate in this present account—but I can't offer any three-dimensional proof of their existence. And I certainly don't believe that when someone dies he or she automatically becomes a ghost. That's nonsense. Ghosts are generally unhappy souls who refuse to move on to the next level after death. And what level is that, you ask? I don't know precisely, but I do know that death is simply a transition, a gateway into another realm, and that we all live many lives as the mysterious cycle continues. (I've been regressed, and found myself drawn back into earlier incarnations when I was a sheriff in the Old West and, centuries before that, an English soldier. I was also a swordsman in the Italian Renaissance and a Greek scholar during the Athenian Golden Age; from those lifetimes I gained both a love of fencing and a decidedly-intellectual approach to life.)

At heart, I'm a skeptic, which is why I got into this game in the first place. When I was a kid, I read about how the late Harry Houdini took a special delight in exposing phony psychics and mediums; he inspired me to follow his example. I enjoy debunking fakes and con artists who prey on a gullible public desperate to contact their departed loved ones.

Most of the cases I've investigated have been hokum. There are, however, exceptions. Cases I can't explain away on a rational basis—and that's when things can get dangerous.

Very dangerous.

*   *   *

November, 1997
Winchester House. The day following Halloween.
She was with the group of tourists being guided through the huge mansion, yet she felt detached, isolated. A sense of engulfment overwhelmed her. She seemed about to be crushed within the confines of this narrow stairway; the walls and ceiling quivered with life. An iced chill entered her body, penetrating her to the bone, a cold that pulsed and throbbed within her, absorbing her essence, taking control of her body.

Utter, total control.

As their male guide, a sandy-haired, brightly-chattering marketing major from San Jose State, led the group of tourists down a dim hallway beyond the stairs, she suddenly veered left, into a closed-off section of the vast mansion. A man followed her, looking confused. Thick-necked, thick-waisted, with a red, sweating face.

"I don't think we're suppose to be in this part of the house," he said.

She turned to him, smiling. Her eyes were opaque black pools, without pupils; a glacial coldness filled them. Her body felt incredibly powerful. Strength lived within her.

"When I saw you leave the others," he said. "I just automatically followed you. Guess I made a mistake."

"You did," she agreed, driving her thumbs into the soft of his neck. He gasped, staggering back, frantically gripping her wrists in a futile attempt to dislodge the killing hands.

A final squeeze. A brutal, wrenching twist. The sound of breaking bones, rending flesh. A sudden eruption of red.

She looked down at the broken corpse.

She was still smiling.

*   *   *

I had an appointment at NBC in Burbank to meet a couple of network producers regarding a paranormal TV series. They'd asked me if I'd be interested in acting as technical advisor on the show. When they named the kind of money they were willing to pay, I told them, sure, I was interested. Considering the fact that I hadn't worked a new case in several weeks, I was *damned* interested.

I drove over to the San Fernando Valley from my place near the ocean in a new Mazda Protégé (metallic silver with red trim). My red Honda was in the shop with a sick transmission, so I'd been given this loaner. It had plenty of pep and style and I enjoyed the way it swallowed the canyon curves on the drive to Burbank.

The bored gate guard waved me through into the NBC visitor parking area and I ambled across the wide asphalt lot toward the administration building. I felt fine, walking under a serene, cloudless California sky with the October sun warming my shoulders. There's nothing on the planet like L.A. weather. That's why I'm a dedicated Angeleno.

After signing in, I reached the end of the main hallway and entered the commissary. The two producers had asked me to meet them here instead of their office because "we get hungry around four, and it's quiet in the commissary after the lunch crowd splits."

At a table near the door, Hud Alkin (slight, bald, thin-lipped) was seated next to Avery Netter (heavy and toothy, with bottle-thick glasses and a veined nose ripe as a strawberry). They were already tucking into big slices of mincemeat pie à la mode.

"Kincaid, is it?" asked Netter.

"I'm your boy," I said as they stood to shake my hand.

"What d'ya want? Pie? Coffee?"

"Nope. I had a late lunch."

I sat down facing them.

"We don't know jack about the paranormal," Netter told me. His eyes swam like bloodshot fish behind the thick lenses. "Our last show was a sitcom with Elly Jenkins."

"Humongous," said Hud Alkin. "Augmented. And a nice tush. But she's a dimwit."

"Show was called *Nine to Fivers*," explained Netter. "All about this dippy chick who worked for a slimeball in Manhattan. He kept trying to lay the make on her and she kept slipping away. Had these two dippy girlfriends and they—"

"Yeah," cut in Alkin. "One of them was a lez, but we had to play it cool in the homo area so's not to piss off the Pat Robertson crowd."

"Show was suppose to be set in New York but we shot it right here in the Valley." said Netter. "Ever watch it?"

"Afraid not," I said. "I don't see much TV. Mostly, it's the late night news or public television. I'm not into sitcoms."

"You didn't miss anything," said Netter. "The show was a bomb."

"Yeah," agreed Alkin. "It sucked."

"We got the axe after our thirteenth episode," said Netter. "Elly blamed us. She was planning on upsizing for the fall season. New implants."

"So what makes you want to produce a paranormal series?" I asked them.

"It's the broad I shack with," said Netter. "She's wacko for all those *Twilight Zone* reruns. Watches them over and over.

Asked me how come we can't do a show like that."

"Yeah," nodded Alkin. "That's when we came up with the idea of doing *Beyond the Beyond*. Nifty, huh?"

"Sounds like a Sinatra oldie," I said. "Has NBC okayed your title?"

"Yeah," nodded Alkin. "They went bonkers for it. Primo potential. Should grab some huge ratings, they say."

"But we don't know jack about the paranormal," repeated Netter. "Which is where you come in."

"Do you have any scripts to show me?" I asked.

"Hell, no," said Alkin. "We thought maybe *you* could do the scripts."

"I'm no TV writer," I said. "You talked about me coming in as a tech advisor. I thought that's what we were here to discuss."

"Yeah," nodded Alkin. "But we changed our minds. Me and Avery, we figger you should write the show."

"Look, I told that you I—"

Alkin clapped me on the shoulder. "Hey, fella, we can *teach* you to write TV. Anybody can do it. Most of the writers in this industry are morons. Can't hardly spell their own names. And you'll be making major bread."

I considered the extra money. "Well...it's a possibility. But I need to be filled in on the overall concept. What's the show about?"

"Who knows?" shrugged Netter. "That's your department. All we got so far is the title."

"And it took us three months to get that," declared Alkin.

I stood up. "There's obviously been a misunderstanding. Let's just forget the whole thing."

"Hey!" Netter said, a whining note in his voice. "We thought you knew all about demons and spooks."

"Seems I know a lot more about them than you do about television," I said. "Ciao, gentlemen."

And I walked out of the commissary.

Driving the Mazda back to my place I buzzed Kelly. She'd moved up in the world—from journalist to fashion writer. Has a cover story in the current issue of *Vogue*. In fact, she'd just returned from a fashion show at the Royal Palace in Monte Carlo. I hadn't seen her in over a month and I missed her. I told her so on the phone.

"What you *really* miss is my cooking," she teased.

"Your shrimp scampi is the stuff that dreams are made of," I admitted.

"You stole that from Huston's *Maltese Falcon*."

"Well, he copped it from Shakespeare."

"Paraphrased it," Kelly corrected me.

I chuckled. "So when do we get together? Can't wait to run my hands up and down your firm Irish body."

"I'm against a tight deadline on the Monaco story," she said. "We can get together on Saturday."

"Today is only Wednesday. Why do I have to wait three days to see you?"

"I'm covering a fashion show this Saturday in Catalina. New Italian designer, Santini. Talented guy. He decided to debut his line on the island this year. Figures. L.A. is now the center of the universe, and exotic Catalina will add that touch of Southern California magic."

"Must I always share you with the public?"

"After the show I'm all yours," said Kelly. "We can spend the whole day together chasing buffalo."

"Didn't know they had buffalo on Catalina."

"They do. Gotta go. I'll phone you later."

And she rang off.

As I unlocked the front door I heard the phone ringing inside the house.

"Kincaid," I said when I reached it.

"Davey!" said a rough male voice on the other end of the line.

"Mike, you old bastard! How the hell are ya?"

"How'd you know it was me?"

"Easy. I never let anyone else call me Davey."

"And I never let anyone else call me an old bastard."

"A year goes by and I don't hear a peep from you," I said. "Now, out of the blue, you phone me. What's wrong?"

"Can't this just be a friendly call?" asked Mike Lucero. "Why does something have to be wrong?"

"Because you only call when you need me. Which is okay. I like to feel needed."

"So, all right, smartass...I do need you. Can you drop by the station?"

"When?"

"*Now!*" he growled. "This is vital."

"To a cop, everything's vital," I said. "What's up?"

"It's Lyn, my youngest sister." He hesitated. "You know how you always say we're all psychic to some degree?"

"That's what I always say."

"Well, I got a...kind of a psychic flash about her. I know she's in trouble big-time. And you can help."

"I'll be there in half an hour," I said.

"Thanks, Davey."

When I pulled off the coast road into the lot at the Malibu Sheriff's Station, Detective Lucero was waiting for me at the entrance. Mike was as big and burly as ever. Football burly. With cop's eyes that bore into you like knife blades. You can always tell a cop by his eyes.

We walked through the station to his back office. Which was, as usual, a total mess—jammed with care reports, stacks of research notes, scattered folders, yellowed newspapers, and vintage pulp magazines (he was partial to *Wu Fang, Detective*).

Past and present mixed together in Mike. He still typed his reports on his ancient Smith-Corona manual, but he was a wiz when he worked with the station computers. Now he took a seat behind his battered oak desk, lit a foul cigar (all of his cigars are foul), and tipped back in his chair.

"I thought you were going to give up the stogies," I said. "Yet here you are, still smoking."

"And here *you* are—still dressed like a damn drugstore cowboy," he growled, referring to my studded cotton shirt, Levi's, and tooled-leather boots.

"At least my outfit won't give me lung cancer."

He grinned at me. Mike enjoyed direct, no B.S. conversation. We'd always talked straight to each other.

I said, "If you want my help, you'll have to kill the stogie. I didn't come over here to die from secondary cigar smoke."

"Okay, okay," he grunted, stubbing out his cheroot in a cracked glass ashtray. "But I want you to know I wouldn't do this for anybody else."

"I'm touched," I said. "Now...what's going on with your sister? What trouble is she in?"

"Let me backtrack some," Mike said. "You need to know what kind of girl Lyn is."

I nodded. "So tell me about her."

"She was my mother's last child. Two weeks later Mama passed on—some infection, I was told. A month later Dad died of a heart attack. I think he just couldn't stand to live without Mama."

"Tough, losing your parents that early," I said. "Hit you hard, I bet."

"Sure, but it hit Lyn a lot harder. She grew up with no memories of her mother or father." Lucero sighed, easing back into his chair. "I can still hear my mother's voice. It was wonderfully soft."

"I know you were raised in one of the northern New Mexico villages," I said. "Did Lyn grow up with you?"

"No," Mike said. "After Dad died, Mama's brother took Lyn to live with his family in Chicago. I never saw her again until she was in her teens, and then only briefly when she visited me during my senior year at the University of New Mexico."

"What was she like back then?"

"Well, she'd just turned thirteen, but she was already beautiful," Lucero declared. "I knew she was going to be—what is that phrase for beautiful women?—drop dead gorgeous. That was Lyn."

"What did she want to be when she grew up?"

"She always hated the idea of marriage, settling down. Didn't want to be a mother. Maybe she thought she'd die, like Mama had. Actually, she wanted to be what you are—a psychic investigator."

Hearing this was a shock. "In all the time we've known each other, you never mentioned that. I had no idea your sister was into the paranormal."

Lucero shrugged. "Just didn't occur to me to tell you."

"Until the Phillips case, you always had contempt for what I did. You called it 'crazy spook stuff.' Remember?"

"Oh sure—and part of that was because of Lyn. I was put off by her obsession with the occult. Figured she was throwing her life away. So you got the rebound. Sorry."

"After her visit to you at the university...how often did the two of you see each other?"

"Hardly at all," he said. "She had her life, and I had mine. Lyn was off on her own at seventeen. Left Chicago and moved to New Orleans. She'd phone at Christmas...send me a postcard now and then. But for the past thirteen months I've heard nothing from her."

"How old is she now?"

"She's thirty four."

"What about your feeling that she's in big trouble...that 'psychic flash' you mentioned?"

Mike had removed a fresh cigar from the humidor on his desk, but he didn't light it, just twisted it around and around in his fingers. Nervously. He was plainly upset.

"Maybe a month ago I began thinking about Lyn," he told me. "Wondering what she was up to, where she was, why she hadn't contacted me in so long. Then, last night, I suddenly woke straight up in bed with this *scene* in my head. So real...so damned real! It shook me so much I couldn't get back to sleep. I almost called you up to tell you about it right then and there—but I didn't want to wake you." He stared at the unlit cigar in his fingers. "Hell, I thought I'd forget it, the way you forget dreams—but the scene didn't go away. It stuck inside my head."

"Describe it," I said.

"It'll sound crazy to you. Doesn't make any sense, really."

"Try me."

He pushed the cigar aside and scrubbed at his lower jaw. His eyes took on a hard shine. "Lyn was in this big place... maybe like a kind of castle...and something was stalking her...closing in on her...something dark and terrible."

"Did it have a form?"

"No, I just...sensed it. But I knew it was really dangerous and that Lyn didn't know it was stalking her, didn't know it was going to..."

"To what?"

"I dunno. It would do something awful to her. Which is when I woke up sweating bullets. Could hardly get my breath. And my heart was thumping bang-bang-bang against my chest."

"What makes you think it wasn't just another nightmare?"

"Believe me, this was no nightmare. It was real...it was a warning—telling me she's in big trouble." He leaned forward, locking his eyes to mine. "I want you to find her, Davey. Find Lyn for me and see if she's okay."

"But you're the cop," I said. "Why send *me* out to find her? Can't you—"

He cut me off, a note of near-panic in his voice. "This is different. You know the paranormal, I don't. I think that she could be into something that only you could handle. Besides, I can't put out an official trace on her. She's not missing, and she's not in any obvious known danger. I'm asking you as a friend—will you help me?"

"You know I will. But I need a starting point. Did she ever get married? Got a husband I could talk to?"

"No marriage—but she had moved to Southern California the last time I heard from her. In '96 she was living with this jazz player, Eddie Chapman...studio musician, he's worked for all the big labels. Lyn was attracted to him because she believed he was Louis Armstrong reincarnated. Both guys played trumpet."

"She still with him?"

"Who knows? She was in '96."

"Where is Chapman now?"

"I heard he was playing horn at a small club in Hollywood. 'The Low Note,' on Vine. When I phoned over there this morning, they told me they never heard of Eddie Chapman; their horn man's name is Tomi Rogers. And that's when I called you."

"The club's a place to start," I said. "Got a picture of your sister?"

"Only a baby picture."

"That won't help. Describe her for me."

He did that. Height. Weight. Eyes. Hair. How she liked to dress. I knew I had all I was going to get from him.

Ten minutes later I was on my way to Hollywood.

*   *   *

December 1997
Generally he worked outside, in the garden, but sometimes, on rare occasions, he needed to go inside the house. The blade of the short-handled spade he was using for the rose bushes on the west side had revealed a leak coming from the house; there had to be a broken pipe under the kitchen sink on the other side of the wall. He needed to turn off the valve before he called the plumber; he didn't want the rose bed flooded. He was quite proud of his work with the roses, which were among the most admired in the Valley area. If she were alive, Miss Sarah would also be proud of them. His grandfather had worked for Miss Sarah and claimed that, although she had a reputation of being rough on her help, she was actually a fine lady of outstanding moral character. Always paid her employees twice the going wage, too.

The sun cast long shadows across the yard as he moved toward one of the side entrance doors. Taking the house key from the pocket of his denim shirt, he inserted it into the lock—then hesitated.

Ever since they found that tourist's body, the day after Halloween, Winchester House had been closed to the public. The police had no clues as to who the killer was, and why he'd torn the man's head off. Terrible way to die! Some odd things had been going on in Winchester House of late—or so he'd been told. The tower bells chiming at midnight...the organ playing in the Grand Ballroom when nobody was inside to play it...drawers suddenly popping open...strange lights flickering in the hallways...a big door flying off its hinges. Somebody even reported seeing the figure of a woman standing at an upper window.

He didn't take much stock in such lurid reports. Personally, he'd never encountered anything unusual around the place despite all the stories people liked to tell. Still, he found himself hesitating at the door. It was stupid. There was nothing to be afraid of. Stupid. He squared his shoulders, turned the key, and stepped inside.

The house was full of late-afternoon shadows spidering up the walls and spreading along the floors and ceilings, creating little pools of darkness in the far corners. And once he'd closed the door behind him he'd felt the silence, like a palpable entity, like something alive. He'd never before thought about silence being alive.

Let's see now...the kitchen he wanted was two hallways down, near a flight of back stairs. He had cleared the front hallway and was halfway through the second when he suddenly stopped, holding his breath. Someone else was inside the house; he was certain he'd heard the sound of footsteps descending the stairs. Odd—because so far as he knew, he was alone here. He strained to listen.

Nothing.

Silence.

He smiled, amused by his nervous reaction. Seems all those weird stories had affected him. Since there was no sound from the kitchen area his nerves must have supplied those footsteps. He felt foolish, childish.

The shadows deepened. Like a wash of dark fog.

He continued, reached the kitchen, faced the stairs. Nothing. No one was there. He moved to the sink and crouched down. Yep, there it was. A slow leak now, but if he hadn't discovered it, the situation could have become much worse. He reached out to shut off the valve.

He was reaching for it when he felt a hard blow on his back, as if he'd been punched. Pain, sharp and savage. And a spreading wetness, soaking the back of his shirt. He stood up and twisted around. An object was protruding be-tween his shoulders. He could see it reflected in the kitchen window.

A knife.

A long-bladed kitchen knife.

Someone chuckled softly from the doorway behind him.

There was a lot of blood.

*   *   *

I found The Low Note just where Mike said I would—half-a-block south from Hollywood Boulevard, on Vine. The club's stained glass windows fronting the street were patterned in horns, drums, and piano keys. A printed sign, taped to the glass, told me when various jazz groups would perform, listing all the star players. Eddie Chapman's name was not among them.

I entered through a batwing saloon door, adjusting my eyes to the interior dimness. Not much business at this time of day. A few dedicated jazz buffs were seated at a scatter of tables in front of a small stage. The music was sweet. An interesting combo: the drummer was thin and chalky with bad teeth; the piano man was black and sassy in cut velvet; the short drink of water on guitar looked stoned; and the horn man had a lean body topped by girl-killer eyes and a crooked nose.

I sat down, ordered a San Pellegrino, and listened.

They were playing "When the Saints Come Marching In," and the horn man *did* remind me of Louis Armstrong. His style was close. Even kept a balled kerchief in one hand, the way Louis always did. He was damned good with a trumpet.

When the set ended I walked up to him. "You know Eddie Chapman?"

"Who's askin'?" He gave me a fishy stare.

"I'm David Kincaid, and I'm trying to locate Chapman."

"You a cop?"

"No."

"What do you want with Eddie?"

"Then you know him?"

"I didn't say so."

"You called him Eddie."

He grinned. "Know who I am?"

"I assume your Tomi Rogers."

He nodded. "People call me 'Checkers.' Because I like the game. Even got me a pocket board. You play checkers?"

"Not for awhile. Played when I was a kid."

"Yeah, people think it's a kid's game, but I take it serious."

"That's fine," I said.

"Is Eddie in trouble?"

"Not that I know about."

"You must have a good reason to wanta talk to him."

"It's about a girl he knows."

"Lyn Lucero?" His eyes darkened. "Is this about Lyn?"

"How come you know her name?"

He gestured toward a corner table. "Sit down. I'm Eddie Chapman."

At the table he told me he'd always hated his name. "It's really *Edgar* Chapman...and who the hell wants to be called Edgar? Like that Tarzan guy. Edgar Rice whatever."

"Burroughs," I said.

"Yeah, him. Bet he hated being called Edgar."

I sipped at my San Pellegrino. Chapman ordered a Foster's.

"So Edgar turned into Eddie, right?"

"Even that didn't help," he said, "so I took my middle name, Thomas, and turned it into Tomi, then added Roy's last name."

"Roy?"

"My idol. From all his old movies I saw on television—Roy

Rogers." He grinned, remembering. "I used to have a cowboy shirt just like the one Roy had on in *Bad Man of Deadwood*. I wore that shirt everywhere. Momma couldn't get it off me. Even slept in that shirt."

"I came here to ask you about Lyn Lucero," I reminded him. "Can we talk about her?"

"Oh, sure. Sure we can." He was fiddling with his brew, sloshing the amber liquid around his glass. "Is she in some kind of trouble?"

"That's what I was hoping you could tell me." I said. "I take it you two have split."

"Yeah," Chapman nodded. "December...almost two years ago. She just packed up and walked."

"Why?"

"Louis Armstrong."

"Her brother said she thought you were his reincarnation."

"Yeah, that's what she thought when we first met. I'd been into boxing as a kid back in Peoria where I grew up. I fought bantamweight. They billed me as 'The Peoria Punisher,' but in the ring I was the one who took all the punishment. That's why my beak is crooked. Had it busted three times. I sure wasn't much of a boxer."

"When did you switch to a horn?"

"I'd always liked to listen to jazz and when Pop bought me a trumpet for my twenty-fourth birthday I took to it like a duck to water. Had what they call a natural talent."

"When did you meet Lyn?"

"In a club. Little joint in Westwood Village. I was playing as Eddie Chapman when she came in one night and asked me to do 'Saints.' Came around after the session, all goggle-eyed. 'I *know* you!' she says. 'You're Louis Armstrong! He's in *your* body. You're him!' She was real excited."

"What did you say to that?"

He grinned. "I said hell, yeah, I was Armstrong. I mean,

when a knockout like Lyn is hot for me, I'll be anybody she wants me to. If she'd said I was Clark Gable I would've said sure, that's me. We made it that same night. Said she was thrilled to be done by a jazz legend."

"So you started living together?"

"Right. I even started playing with a balled-up handkerchief in my hand—the way Armstrong did. He used it to wipe the sweat off his face. Got to be a trademark of mine, so I still carry it."

"Exactly what caused Lyn to walk out on you?"

"Like I said, it was Armstrong." He sipped his beer. "Lyn told me she'd gone to a medium who contacted Armstrong's spirit, and the frigging ghost told her I was a phony, that he hadn't reincarnated in anybody. That cooked it. She accused me of lying to her, of pretending to be somebody I wasn't—so she split."

"Heard from her since?"

"Naw. But an actor came into the club about a month after she left and told me she'd hooked up with a director at Universal. Dude by the name of Ben Dunston."

"Did the actor tell you why she picked Dunston?"

"He told me that the guy made horror movies and so Lyn figured he was in touch with the supernatural. That's why she latched onto him."

"They still together?"

Chapman shrugged. "Maybe. Maybe not. Like I said, she never contacted me after she split. But you could find out."

"I'll do that," I said. I stood up and we shook hands. "Appreciate your help, Ed."

"Call me Checkers," he said.

At Universal, I asked the gate guard about Ben Dunston. The guard made a quick phone call, then sent me in, to a man named Alexander Dickey in Administration. I was told to park along the fence in front of Sound Stage 4. A red bulb was lit above the side door which indicated an inside shoot.

"They're doin' one of them Billy the Kid things in there," a stagehand told me as I got out of the Mazda. "Scene where the Kid breaks outta jail an' kills a deputy with a shotgun. Blows him smack in half. Blam! Blam! Double barrel. You like Westerns?"

"I liked *Butch Cassidy and the Sundance Kid* on video," I said.

"Yeah," nodded the stagehand. "Loved the train scene where they blew the door off the baggage car. Pieces of wood and paper money flying ever which way. Remember what Newman said?"

"Uh...no. No, I don't."

"He grins and he says, 'Think you used enough dynamite there, Butch?' That was a real hoot, with all the money flyin' through the air an'—"

"The administration building is ahead and to the left, isn't it?" I asked, just to shut him up.

"That's where it is," he said.

I reached the wide bricked patio in front of Administration and looked up at the building. A towering mass of stone and black glass that somehow made me think of an Egyptian tomb.

Third Floor. Suite 306. A small bronze plaque on the door told me this was the right office.

ALEXANDER J. DICKEY
PRODUCTION

I walked inside and the receptionist, obviously a regular on the Nautilus machines, asked me if I had an appointment. "No, I just came here to ask about a director who'd worked for the studio. Mr. Dickey is supposed to be able to help me."

"Oh yes, Pete phoned about you."

I raised an eyebrow.

"The gate guard. He said he was sending you over here." She turned to press a button on the front of her desk. "I'll see if Mr. Dickey can talk to you."

He could.

"Go right in," she said, nodding toward an inner door.

Alex Dickey, middle-aged and potbellied, dressed in a full golfing outfit including the cap, was standing in the middle of his office, putting. He'd laid a wide strip of Astroturf over the rug and was about to send a small white golf ball into a cup sunk into the far edge of the mat. He tried the shot, and missed.

"Damn!" he said under his breath, leaning to retrieve the ball. "I'm pretty good with the long shots, but when I'm putting, I stink!"

"Sorry to hear that," I said.

He laid his putter aside, and sat down in a high-back chair by his desk. Studio execs are usually unbelievably busy during their long working hours; many of them routinely do a hundred or more phone calls a day, in addition to conferences, script and treatment reading, and analysis of the former week's grosses. Dickey's freedom to perfect his golf stroke told me that he was well on the other side of the power he'd obviously once enjoyed; he probably had a relative on Universal's Board of Directors who was protecting his paycheck until he'd finished the years he needed for full retirement.

"Guess you think I look funny in these clothes," he said.

"Hey, to each his own. A pal of mine just accused me of dressing like a drugstore cowboy."

"Makes me a feel like I'm out there...you know, on the green. Puts me in the right mood," he said.

"I understand," I told him, sitting down on a red-leather couch.

He stared at me. "Who are you and what do you want?"

"David Kincaid. I'm trying to locate a director named Dunston."

"Why?"

"He was, or is, involved with a woman I'm tracking, Lyn Lucero."

"Never heard of her. An actress?"

"No. She's not in the business."

"One of Ben's chippies, eh?"

I didn't like his tone or the smirk on this face, but I repressed my irritation. Mouthing off wouldn't get me what I needed.

"I'd appreciate your telling me where I can reach Dunston."

"And I'd appreciate your getting the hell out of my office."

He stood up, walked to the door and pulled it open, glaring at me.

"I don't understand. What did I say to—"

"Ben Dunston is a talentless little turd who directed three turkeys in a row for us, and then had the nerve to sue us for a bonus. We told him to stuff it."

"All I want to know is—"

"Scram!" snapped Alex Dickey. He sounded like Humphrey Bogart.

The redhead in the outer office felt sorry for me. She'd been listening to our talk on her intercom. She silently motioned me over to her desk, leaned close, and whispered in my ear: "Colma. Ben's in Colma on a werewolf shoot."

"Thanks," I said.

And I had my lead.

*   *   *

June, 1998
His parents had called him a bum and kicked him out at

sixteen. After he'd already been expelled from High School in San Leandro, California, and after he'd put a bun in Nancy Stafford's oven. When her old man found out, he'd threatened to kill him, which is when his folks said they'd had enough and wanted him out.

Okay, fine. Who gave a rat's ass? His parents were a couple of lousy drunks, sucking the bottle every day, and who were they to call him a bum? Pot calling the kettle black.

He holed up across the Bay in Frisco, at a pal's apartment on Post, trying to figure out a way to keep alive. Damned if he'd get a job. He wasn't going to push burgers across a counter or pick up other people's trash or work on the wharf with a lot of smelly fish. Not him. Those jobs were for suckers or lamebrains.

He had a summer job once, in a paper box factory. His stacks kept tipping over and the foreman got pissed and fired him. He got even for that. Slashed all four tires on the foreman's new Chevy.

He and his pal decided to try selling crack, but it didn't pan out because the law raided their stash and arrested his pal. He made it to the roof and jumped to the next building and got away clean, but it had been close.

So pushing drugs was a no-go. Too risky. He didn't want to end up in the slammer. The landlord of the apartment house on Post gave the cops his description so he sent a note to the creep telling him he planned to blow up the building. Just a bluff. But he could have done it if he'd wanted to. The reason he got expelled from school was because he brought in a stick of dynamite he'd copped from a construction site and set it off in the gym. Made a huge hole in the floor. The explosion rocked the whole school.

He tried some minor shoplifting and learned to be pretty good as a pickpocket. Snatched an old broad's purse once on Market. She near had a stroke. Screamed her guts out and flopped around like a beached whale. Comic sight. But this kind of stuff was a waste of time. Burger money. That's all it brought in. Piss-poor way to make a living.

Which is when he started to burglarize rich-bitch houses around the Bay. This was more like it! Right on! He made some awesome scores: loose cash, rings, gold watches, silver tea pots, even some antiques he got a good price for. Amazing what these chumps left around in plain sight. Cleaning out their houses was a cinch. Pop in a side window, scoop up the goodies, then out again. Just like that old radio guy his gramps told him about—the Shadow. That was him. Nobody ever saw him, let alone caught him. He'd case each joint to make sure the owners were out before he broke into the place. And he knew how to fix the alarms. It was easy. Exciting, too. Gave him a real high, doing it.

In Berkeley, after he'd done a house there, he met a girl in a local bar. She was a little tramp, but she knew how to screw.

They were in this motel and he woke up in the middle of the night to find her going through his wallet for cash. That cut it. He left her sprawled face-down on the bed. She wouldn't be screwing anyone else for awhile. If ever.

Finally he got bored with Frisco. He wanted to try his new vocation in another locale. He thought he was good enough to do some of those rich houses down in L.A. Yeah, Los Angeles was ripe for his kind of talent, and he'd be away from the fog down there. Damn fog in Frisco was killing him. He hated it.

But first, before heading downcoast to L.A., he decided to take a little side trip a few miles south, to San Jose. Center of Silicon Valley, where every computer geek was a friggin' multimillionaire! There must be hundreds of rich houses just ripe for the picking there, he knew. But first he wanted to see this one house that had belonged to a batty old dame who kept building new sections on it her whole life because some ghost told her to.

The TV said the house had been closed recently after somebody died in it. So there it sat, just waiting for a guy like him to claim all the goodies inside. No telling what kind of stuff was in there, but he'd soon find out.

Oh yeah, Winchester House would be easy pickings.

Towers and cornices and turrets and balconies and cupolas...Jeez, the place looked like some kind of big wooden castle. And it was spread out all over hell and gone. The old dame had really built herself something wild here. The stained-glass windows alone had to be worth a fortune. Place must be full of treasures. A real windfall for him. He felt very lucky. God was smiling on him.

It was a little after midnight and real quiet. He'd slipped over the outside wall and was standing on the front lawn facing the cut-glass entrance doors. The night guard who was patrolling the grounds was out of sight, walking around in the back somewhere. And there didn't seem to be any guards inside. No lights or movement. The place was wide open, just begging to be taken.

The Shadow strikes again! Winchester House stripped of valuables! Famous mansion successfully burglarized! Police baffled!

Ha! What a sweet set-up.

He moved around to the left side of the vast structure, keeping an eye out for the guard. Found a lower window that he could jimmy. Piece of cake. Got it open in nothing flat.

So far, so good.

Inside, he used a small pin flash to scout the area, shielding the light with his other hand. Lots of fancy wallpaper and carved wood. Polished peg flooring. Heavy drapes shutting out the moonlight.

Jeez, but it had suddenly turned *cold* in here! Icy cold. Like he'd walked into a fridge. And...although this was crazy...things were *moving*. The walls seemed to ripple, making him dizzy. The ceiling shifted. A big cabinet tipped toward him, crashing down. Startled, he dropped the pin-light, then began groping for it in the sudden blackness.

His hand touched something familiar. *Flesh!* Somebody was on the floor right at his feet! The figure sat up, and one of its icy hands caught him by the throat. He choked, tried to scream, but couldn't. Desperately, he flung himself back, his fists battering at the thing that gripped him.

No use.

Choking me.

Can't breathe.

He was picked up and thrown against a stone fireplace with incredible force. He felt his bones snap, his skin split. Then...

No more breath.

No more life.

* * *

On Thursday morning I drove north to Colma. It's a small community ten miles south of San Francisco, and it's known in California as "The City of the Dead." That was the title of the TV documentary I'd seen about it, and maybe Ben Dunston had seen it, too. More than three million dead rested in Colma: they were capped in bronze urns, shelved in white-stone mausoleums, and buried under marble slabs in the town's sixteen cemeteries. With a population of less than 1500, the dead vastly outnumber the living in Colma.

I could understand why a fright-film director such as

Dunston would figure he'd found a peachy place to shoot his werewolf film.

Colma had inherited a large number of its deceased occupants. In the late 1930s, the San Francisco city fathers decided to convert the municipal cemeteries into land development projects. They dug up thousands of graves and shipped the remains ten miles south, to Colma. A number of celebrities, from sugar tycoons to potato chip moguls, are now buried there, including newspaper magnate William Randolph Hearst, Tombstone marshal Wyatt Earp, and stunt flier Lincoln Beachey, along with (as the old-timer on TV recounted) "circus clowns, Alcatraz inmates, bartenders, nuns, bridge builders, long-shoremen, and Hell's Angels."

I remember the documentary's camera homing in on a very special cemetery known as "Pet's Rest." Tiny gravestones mark the passage of iguanas, cheetahs, goldfish, monkeys, parrots, hoot owls, guinea pigs, pet lizards, and assorted fur-bearing creatures. Tina Turner's dog, wrapped in one of the pop star's fur coats, is buried in Pet's Rest, along with a dead poodle with a full set of gold teeth, and a beloved horse, still wearing its bridle and saddle.

Since my Honda wasn't ready yet, I drove up to Colma in the Mazda, thinking a lot about Lyn Lucero on the way. Obviously, we both shared an abiding fascination with the paranormal. The difference is that I am careful to maintain a position of objective skepticism (unless the phenomena proves to be genuine, which it does sometimes), whereas Lyn obviously accepted the whole world of the supernatural at face value, without questioning its essential validity.

At least that was what Mike told me in the parking lot at Malibu Station just before I left. He talked, in frustration, about Lyn's total obsession with vampires, ghouls, demons, psychics, UFOs, magic, mediums, reincarnation, haunted houses, and all things occult. It began in her young childhood in Chicago when she'd wake up from a nightmare and think it was real. Nothing her Uncle Frank could say to her would convince her that she'd just been dreaming. Dreams, for Lyn Lucero, were a dark reality that haunted her.

"According to what Uncle Frank told me, she read nothing but horror stories from age ten," Mike had declared. "By twelve, she'd read everything H.P. Lovecraft had ever written. Christmas was okay, but Halloween was her favorite holiday. She played a witch in the seventh-grade school play, and claimed afterwards that she could fly on a broomstick if she wanted to. And maybe she really believed it. Other little girls played with Barbie. Lyn traded her lunch money for voodoo dolls, which she bought from classmates whose families were from the Caribbean. Whenever she was irritated with a teacher, she stuck a pin in her teacher's doll. I tell you, Davey, she was a strange little thing."

With these thoughts about Mike's sister running in my head I drove through downtown Colma, passing a fried chicken hut, a Circle-K, a medium-sized grocery store, and a dilapidated motion picture theater with a large FOR LEASE sign on its marquee. In the modern mall-world of multi-screens, this downtown film house had become as outdated as a buggy whip.

I pulled into a Shell station to gas up the Mazda and get some directions. In a town this small, a Hollywood film crew was bound to attract a lot of attention.

"Oh, yeah, they're shootin' right here in Colma," the age-bent station man said. He was white-haired and whiskery and smelled of dust and tobacco. "Whole passel of trucks an' trailers and what all. I wanted to try out to play me a corpse in the movie, but I'm stuck here at the station, worse luck."

"Where are they shooting today?" I asked him. "Where can I find them?"

The old man pointed directly ahead. "Stay on the street

and keep a'goin' for half mile or so, then take a right at the Toys R Us and go straight from there. You'll run smack into Woodlawn, an' that's where they're at."

He grinned like a schoolboy with a nasty secret. "Hear tell they brought their own fake werewolf with 'em—all the way from Hollyweird. They didn't need to. We got us plenty of *real* ones right here in Colma."

"Do you believe in werewolves?"

He nodded vigorously. "Betcha boots I do! I mean. I never actual *seen* one myself, but I been told about 'em. Ever time there's a full moon, they go huntin' in the boneyards. Guess they favor bein' near dead folks."

"Thanks for your help," I said, getting back into the Mazda.

The old man's directions were accurate, and I parked just outside the gate at Woodlawn Cemetery. Crew trucks were strung out along the main road leading into the graveyard, and when I asked a trucker about Ben Dunston, he told me to just keep on walking and I'd find him at the end of the road.

I walked past soot-darkened mausoleums and statues of hovering angels, along rows of time-faded tombstones, several embedded with glass cases set into the stone, displaying religious icons and plastic photos of the deceased.

A marble jack-in-the-box sat atop a child's grave and I paused to read the carved inscription:

TIMOTHY ALLEN HARTWELL

1990-1992

PLUCKED TOO SOON FROM

OUR LOVING EMBRACE

WE MISS YOU, TIMMY BOY

A pot of wildflowers had been placed at the foot of the

marker. The pot had cracked and the flowers had wilted.

I walked on toward the action ahead of me. Cameras. Sound equipment. Lights. Aluminum reflectors. A food truck. Dressing trailers. And an Andy Gump for the crew.

A uniformed cop stopped me, finger to his lips. Shooting in progress. I was to stay put and remain quiet.

Ben Dunston, a bearded, intense man in a baseball cap, sunglasses, a yellow polo shirt, and Levis, was directing a scene in which the werewolf leaped from the branches of a tree upon a terrified teenager, threw her to the ground in front of an open mausoleum, and ripped her blouse away with his sharp, furry paws.

"Cut! Cut!" yelled Dunston. He turned to the werewolf. "What's wrong, Wilbur?"

"It's no good!" complained the wolfguy. "I'm suppose to rip away her blouse so we can appreciate her attributes, right?"

"Right," nodded Dunston.

"Well, lookie here!" He held up his hairy paws. "They sewed the friggin' claws in *upside down!*"

"Wardrobe!" shouted Dunston. A freckled-faced young woman ran toward him. "Get me a new set of wolf paws. Chop-chop!"

I figured it was a good time to approach Dunston as he slumped into his canvas-backed director's chair. His name had been misspelled on the back of the chair: BEN DUSTON. They'd left out the "n."

"Hi," I said, extending my hand. "I'm David Kincaid."

He looked at me, then looked at my hand. "So?"

"So I'd like to talk to you."

"Then talk. You got maybe five minutes."

"I'm told you've been seeing a woman named Lyn Lucero."

"Seeing?" He blinked at me. "You mean *screwing*, don't you? And it's past tense."

"Then you and Lyn are no longer an item?"

"You got it, pal. She's yesterday's news. Haven't seen her since the summer of '97." He stared up at me, a hostile glint in his eyes. "How come you know about me and Lyn?"

"An ex-friend of hers put me onto you," I said. "Told me Lyn thought you were in touch with the supernatural."

Dunston laughed harshly. "Well, that's what she thought. Ha! Just because I make these horror cheapies. She came on strong." He laughed again. "So I took her, as they say, under my wing."

"What happened?" I asked. "Why did she leave?"

"What's your game, pal?" he asked. "Why should I answer your damn questions?"

"I'm helping out Lyn's brother. He's a cop in Malibu. Wants to know what happened to his sister."

He shrugged. "What happened to her is she found out I didn't have any spook connections—that I'm just a guy trying to hustle a buck from the creepos who freak for horror flicks. They pay to see vampires and ghouls and werewolves, so that's what I provide. I give 'em their B and B."

"B and B?"

"Blood and Boobs," said Dunston.

The wolfguy padded over to Ben, holding out his paws. His claws were now correctly placed, long and sharp-looking. "How are these?" he asked, his voice muted by the wolf mask.

Dunston examined the new paws. "They're swell, Willie," he said. "Just make sure you don't scratch her attributes."

"I'll be careful," said the wolf.

Dunston stood up, stretching. He yawned, tugging at the brim of his baseball cap. "Talk's over. I gotta go back to work."

I caught his arm. "Where is she? That's all I need from you—an address."

"She read about this haunted room in the Coronado Hotel. Wanted to see if she could connect with the spook they're supposed to have there. Some book she picked up had a chapter in it about this special haunted hotel room. So off she goes. Who knows where she is by now."

"Obliged," I said. "I'll check it out."

"Okay then," he said.

"One last question."

"What?"

"Why are you doing the werewolf scene in broad daylight? I thought werewolves only came out at night, under a full moon."

"We're shooting day for night," he said. "We'll filter the sunlight, then stick in the moon during post-production. Okay?"

I nodded. "Okay."

And he walked back to the wolf who had new paws.

San Diego was a long drive downcoast from Colma so I decided I'd break up the trip by returning home to Malibu. I'd spend the night there, then drive on to San Diego in the morning.

Where the road ends at Cottontail Ranch my place is just to the right, down a small incline. Surrounded by trees. The feel of wilderness country. Pine, sagebrush, and—on a windy day—the faint salt smell of the Pacific.

It was good to be back in my little world again, which is how I think of my house. With my books and music and art around me like old friends.

There was a message on my answering machine: "Hey, lover! Remember Saturday. I am!"

Kelly, reminding me of our date on Catalina. It had definitely been on my mind during my drive from Colma. I was looking forward to Kelly's company, and it would be a nice break on a case that seemed to be leading me nowhere.

I ate a late dinner and tried to watch some TV, but even PBS was a bummer. I tried to get into a novel I was reading by Flannery O'Connor which she wrote just before she died at 39. Too young. She'd been a helluva writer.

I never met Ms. O'Connor, but we share (shared in her case) a mutual love of peacocks. She raised them; I have several books about them and an original oil painting of one in my den, fantail proudly spread in a glittering array of colors.

All of which leads up to my nightmare.

I couldn't watch anymore television, and I couldn't stay with the O'Connor novel (I actually prefer her short stories), so I gave up and went to bed.

Then the dream took hold of me...

I was alone on a vast stretch of beach. Like the Sahara Desert. Sunwashed dunes rippled away from me toward sandy horizons.

A television set with a black screen was about fifty feet to my left, and a peacock was standing on it. A truly beautiful bird, fantail spread in proud display.

I walked over to it. "Who are you?" (Somehow I knew it could talk. The way you know things in dreams.)

"I'm Lyn," it said. "You've been looking for me."

I nodded. I was naked and the hot sand was burning the soles of my feet. I kept shifting from one leg to the other.

"Are you surprised to have found me?" the bird asked.

"No," I said. "I always find what I look for. That's my job. I'm an investigator."

"Like Sam Spade?"

"No, he was a private detective. I'm not that."

"You're turned on," the peacock said. "Is it because of me?"

"I don't think so," I told the bird. "I don't find you sexually attractive."

"I thought you found peacocks beautiful."

"Oh, yes...you *are* beautiful—but not in a sexual way. And, of course, as a peacock, you're a male."

"Do you watch television?" the bird asked.

"Not often," I said. "There's not much on that's worth watching. I *hate* sitcoms."

"Why don't you switch this set on. You'll be fascinated by what you see."

"It's not connected," I said. "It won't work."

"Yes it will," insisted the bird. "Just try it."

"Okay." I pushed the "ON" button.

It was suddenly ink-black around us, and the screen glowed like a blue beacon.

"Got dark awfully fast," I said.

"Yes," agreed the peacock. "It's that way in the desert. Light one minute, dark the next."

The bird hopped down to stand beside me. "Let's watch," it said.

A newscast was on. The anchor man stared out at us and said: "Well, there's good news tonight. David Kincaid has finally located Lyn Lucero, but she's turned into a peacock which is going to be a shock to her brother, homicide detective, Michael Lucero." The anchor shuffled some papers in front of him and paused for dramatic effect. "The big question tonight is: Will she *stay* in bird form—or will she change again? And into *what*? No one knows."

The picture died; and the screen was a square of fuzzy white, illuminating the area around us.

I looked at Lyn, but the bird was gone. A tall, shaggy beastman stood next to me in the sand. His eyes were glowing red, his teeth like daggers.

Werewolf!

And no Ben Dunston fake, either.

I twisted around and tried to run, but the sand was thick

and unyielding and I floundered to my knees. A clawed hand snapped my neck back, and I felt razor teeth sink deep into the flesh of my neck.

Which is when I woke up. I was shouting and gripping at my throat with both hands. My body was shuddering and soaked in sweat, and my heart was thudding in my chest like a jackhammer.

I got up, walked into the kitchen and fixed some herbal tea. It always relaxes me.

Sitting there at the kitchen table, sipping hot tea and honey, I told myself: the nightmare was trying to communicate something to me. Dreams are the bridge between our superconsciousness and our conscious minds; they're often meaningful and full of wisdom, but their symbols can be difficult to decipher.

Perhaps the message in this one was that Lyn had changed; she was no longer the sister Mike remembered.

Changed? The TV newsman's question haunted me: Into *what*?

I would find out.

And what I eventually found would prove more terrifying than any nightmare.

A bright, clear Friday morning. No clouds. Sky, a hot blue sheet stretching across California. I was on Interstate 5, heading south for Coronado. The tape deck was playing Willie Nelson's *On the Road Again* and I was singing along.

Appropriate. Seems I was on the road a lot in this case, chasing down leads, rolling from one city to another in my Mazda loaner. As the peacock said, "like Sam Spade." But even the Maltese Falcon seemed easier to find than Lyn Lucero.

An unpleasant fluttering in my solar plexus told me this job was not going to end happily. My psychic sense was kicking in and I didn't like what I was being told.

Trouble ahead.

Danger.

Darkness.

Or maybe it was just a sour stomach from the eggs, potatoes, and coffee at Denny's. One of my current goals was to
give up coffee; among many other negative things, it acidi-
fies your system, which is a plenty bad thing to do. I gave up
smoking before I entered my twenties, and I know my lungs
are very grateful. Coffee is the next to go. And that's a promise, I told myself.

When I arrived in downtown San Diego I was reminded
of how much the city had changed since I'd first shipped out
of there back in my Navy days. The whole downtown section had undergone a massive facelift, proving that no matter how ugly a city can be (and San Diego had been *ugly*), it
can be reborn with a lot of effort and proper funding. The
Good Fairy had been looking out for San Diego. Now it was
a showplace of successful civic development.

The long bridge to Coronado Island was freshly painted
and practically free of traffic. My destination, the Hotel del
Coronado on Orange Avenue, was at the far end of the island, with its beach facing the Pacific. It was a world-famous
historical landmark. I'd read enough about it to know that it
was one of the world's great seaside resort hotels. Built sometime in the 1880s, it had hosted kings and scoundrels alike.

I'd heard that eleven U.S. Presidents had slept at the
del Coronado, and that the Prince of Wales met his future
dutchess at a gala in the Grand Ballroom. Several movies had
been filmed here, featuring stars like Douglas Fairbanks and
Marilyn Monroe.

I parked in the lot and walked toward the wide brass entrance doors. The big, wooden, eight-sided Victorian structure towered above me, five stories high, painted a dazzling

white, with rows of bay windows reflecting the westering afternoon sun.

Writer Richard Matheson (a pal of mine who is fascinated by investigations of the paranormal) had set one of his best novels here, *Bid Time Return*. They made a movie about it, called *Somewhere in Time*, starring Christopher Reeve and Jane Seymour. A fantasy. About a modern guy who falls in love with a long-dead actress who'd once performed at the hotel. In my opinion, it was one of Reeve's finest films before his accident with the horse.

I introduced myself at the reception desk to a pinch-faced clerk, Theodore, and asked about Lyn Lucero. Had she registered here in the past?

"*How* past?"

"Last year," I said. "In the summer. Maybe June, July...August."

The clerk smiled indulgently, telling me there was no way he could access that information. Against hotel policy to give out any data on the guests. "Are you with the police?" he wanted to know.

"In a way," I said. "I'm working for a member of the Sheriff's Department in Malibu, a homicide cop. Looking for his sister. I'm almost certain she was a guest at this hotel."

Theodore studied my face, trying to tell if I was putting him on. "I should contact the manager and let him—"

"I'll be very careful with the registration books," I promised. "You can watch me the whole time. I'll sit right over there." I indicated a deep leather chair in the center of the lobby.

He shook his head. "This may be a historic hotel, mister, but we've entered the modern age along with everybody else. No more registration books. We use a *computer*."

"Then that makes it simple. Would you please access the name 'Lyn Lucero'?"

He keyboarded the name. "Yep, August 1997," he said. Almost fourteen months ago.

"Were you on the desk back then?" I asked him.

"No," said Theodore. "I've only been here since last Christmas."

"I need to talk to whoever was on the desk in August of '97," I said.

"That would be Harry Bannister. He got promoted to night manager."

"Where is he now?" I asked.

"Well...he lives right here, in the hotel."

"Can you buzz his room?"

"Harry's usually asleep at this hour, since he works all night. But I suppose I *could* wake him."

"I'd appreciate it," I said. "This is important."

He rang Bannister's room. Waited, then got him on the line, telling him who I was and what I wanted. Then he replaced the receiver onto the console.

"Room 3301. Third floor. The elevator's to your left. Harry's waiting for you."

"Theodore, you're a prince," I said, heading for the elevator.

When Harry Bannister opened the door, his eyes were sleep-fogged and he needed a shave. In rumpled pajamas, with his hair wild and uncombed, he looked to be in his sixties, with a mottled, fleshly face and thin lips.

"Sorry to wake you," I said, telling him my name. "But I felt it was vital."

He waved me into the room—a small suite, actually, with its own kitchenette and a large old-fashioned bathroom.

"Want a cold beer?" he asked. "When I wake up, I always have myself a cold beer."

"Thanks, but I'm fine," I said, taking a chair near the window. Harry had opened the heavy drapes and I could see a stretch of beach outside, bathers dotted along the sand. The ocean was leisurely rolling in, in no hurry since it had been doing the same thing for millions of years.

Bannister got a bottle of Molson's out of the fridge and uncapped it, then sat down on the couch and took a long swallow. "Now what's so 'vital,' Mr. Kincaid?"

"I'm tracing a woman who stayed at this hotel about fourteen months ago," I told him. "You were on the desk then, so you must have signed her in."

"I've signed in a helluva lot of people over the years. Unless they look hinky, I don't pay much attention. They come and go." He pursed his lips. "Name?"

"Lyn Lucero."

He shook his head. "Don't recall."

"Beautiful. Dark hair. Trim figure."

"This is God's country, Mr. Kincaid. Every other female who registers could be the cover girl for next year's *Sports Illustrated* swimsuit edition. What makes Lyn Lucero special?"

"She's heavily into the occult," I explained. "She came here because she read about a haunted room at the del Coronado."

Harry Bannister rubbed the bridge of his nose.

"Yeah...*now* I remember her. She was gung-ho to rent our haunted room. Real intense about it. Like she *had* to sleep in that room."

"Is there a resident ghost here at the hotel?"

He tipped back his head and laughed softly. "Some people sure seem to think so. Me, I figure it's all a lot of malarkey."

"What actually happened in that room?"

He drew in a long breath. "You want the whole story?"

"Please."

He took another hit of the Molson's, crossed his legs, and settled back into the cushions. "Lot of what I'm gonna tell you was found out about later, after the law dug into the case."

"I understand."

"There was a woman who called herself Lottie Bernard. She signed the register that way, but her real name was Kate Morgan. She was a train hustler."

"What's that?"

"Somebody who hustles the suckers. Kate was married to this gambler, Tom Morgan, a real sharpie. Apparently, he could make a deck of cards stand up and take a bow. And the great thing was, from his standpoint, he had this 'innocent' look that made people trust him. Dressed like a yokel and talked that way. Insisted that everybody call him Tommy."

"I get the picture."

"Anyway, him and Kate, who pretended to be his sister, they worked the cross-country trains as a team. She'd flirt with some rich guy who was traveling alone and lure him into a 'friendly' card game with Morgan. The rich guy would always end up losing his shirt, with Kate and Tom stepping off at the next station with all of his money—or at least as much as he had on him, and a lot of those boys traveled with a sizable wad."

"So they were both successful crooks."

"You got it," said Harry Bannister. "Slick as glass, they were. Well, turns out that Tom got Kate pregnant, but he didn't want to be a father. A kid would slow him down, ruin his business. They had a major fight over it. When she refused to get an abortion, he threw her out. She ended up renting a room here at the hotel."

"What year was this?"

"Late November of 1892. She'd bought herself a gun and some cartridges that same week, and had the gun with her when she registered. She was put in room 302, on this floor. Nowadays the number is 3312, but it's the same room." He finished the last of his beer, walked into the kitchen, and tossed the empty bottle into a recycling container.

"Was anyone at the hotel aware that she had a gun?"

"Heck no. She kept it in her purse." He crossed to the couch and settled back into it. "Her being alone and pregnant the way she was...well, that made her real unhappy. Guess she figured there was no future for her. Without a husband, and with no way to make a living for herself and the kid. So she shot herself in the head."

"And her body was found in the room?"

"In a big pool of blood. Ruined the carpet. Hotel had to have it replaced. Her suicide got a lot of press coverage, which the hotel didn't welcome, of course. That's when the newspaper writers poked into her background and found out who she really was and all the rest of it."

"When did the 'haunting' begin?"

"Not long after. People who rented the room claimed they heard footsteps in the middle of the night—like somebody pacing back and forth. And the sound of a woman crying. One old guy woke up at 3 a.m. to see this figure at the foot of the bed, staring at him. Dressed in fancy Victorian clothes— just like Kate wore when she shot herself." He sighed. "Then there was the thing with the mirrors."

"What was that?"

He tugged at a fold of loose flesh under his chin. "Every room in the hotel has a big mirror over the dresser and an- other in the bathroom. After Kate Morgan's death, the mir- rors in that room both cracked, like they'd been in an earth- quake. New ones were put in. *They* cracked. And no matter how many times the mirrors were replaced, the new ones would always get big cracks. Finally, the hotel just gave up. To this day, that room is the only one in the hotel without mirrors."

"And Lyn knew all about this?"

"Sure did. She had this book with her, *Haunted Houses in California*. It had a chapter about the ghost of Kate Morgan. Your lady had it all down by heart—and she insisted on being put in room 3312, so I said okay, and that's where we put her."

"Did she hear the footsteps?" I asked him. "Did she see Kate's ghost?"

"Nope." Bannister chuckled. "And it really pissed her off. She stayed in that room for a full week—even took her meals there—and didn't hear or see a damn thing. Got mad as hell with me. Claimed I'd put her in the wrong room. But when she verified the number out of that book, she had to admit it was sure enough the one Kate Morgan died in."

"When Lyn checked out," I said, "did she leave a forwarding address?"

"No. She just walked away, real disappointed."

"You wouldn't have any idea of where she might have gone?"

"I sure wouldn't," said Harry Bannister.

It was Mike's day off at the station so when I got back to L.A., I drove out to his place in the west San Fernando Valley in Woodland Hills. He lives with his wife, Carla, and their twin daughters off Valley Circle, within drum-range of El Camino Real High School. He's always complaining that early band practice wakes him up on his days off and then he's never able to get back to sleep.

Mike met me at the door in his swimming trunks. Looked good, but he was putting on a bit of heft around his middle. Lucero gained weight easily and was always fighting to keep trim.

The interior of his house, a white one-story ranch type, was in sharp contrast to the cluttered chaos of his office in Malibu. The place had that perpetual "ready for the *Archi-*

tectural Digest photographer" look. His cop's salary was obviously spent with skill and care.

"You can credit Carla for all this," he said, as I mentioned how nice everything looked. "She's a fanatic housekeeper. Disorder is her worst enemy. If I'm in a chair reading the paper and I put it down to go take a leak, it's in the recycling bin by the time I get back. I love her dearly, but she can drive me right up the wall."

"If she runs out of work around here, you can send her to my place. It could use a major cleanup."

Mike grunted. "You always tell me what a mess my office is," he said. "Well, it retaliation—for having to live like this at home."

"Where *is* Carla?" I asked.

"She took the girls to a movie at the Promenade. They're watching some dumb picture about a mouse being chased by a squad of Mafia hit men because the mouse has something they're after. God knows what a mouse could have that the Mafia would want, but that's movies for you. The girls *love* mice. They'll go see anything with a mouse in it."

We sat down in his spotless living room on some oyster-beige upholstered chairs. Carla had good taste.

"I take it you haven't found Lyn," Mike said.

"No, but I've sure tried." I told him about the trail I'd followed from the jazz club in Hollywood to the ghost at the Hotel del Coronado. "I've hit a blank wall. No more leads on where she might be right now."

"You gave it your best shot," he said, "and I want you to know how grateful I am, how much I appreciate the way you've busted your ass for me. You're the real stuff, Davey, and I'll never forget what you tried to do."

"Hey," I protested with a grin. "You make it sound like the hunt's over."

"Well, isn't it?"

"Hell, no. I'm a stubborn bastard and I never give up. I just keep pushing."

"Pushing where?" he asked. "There's nowhere else to go."

"I refuse to believe that," I told him. "People don't just vanish off the face of the earth. Lyn is out there somewhere, and I'm going to find her. My personal crusade."

"What can I say?"

"You don't have to say anything. Just give me a little help."

"How?"

"It's an idea I want to follow up. That's why I came out here, instead of phoning you. I needed to come to your house."

"For what? You got something special in mind?"

"Remember Irene Hopwood?"

"Uh...no, not really."

"Lives in downtown L.A. Big, renovated Victorian house. The psychic. The one with the genuine gift."

"Oh, yeah. Now I remember," nodded Mike. "She helped you on the Phillips case."

"Right," I said. "Driving back from Coronado I was trying to figure a way to get back on Lyn's trail. I was like the outlaw who's chased into a box canyon and looks for a way out. That was me, boxed but still looking."

"So what did you come up with?"

"Irene Hopwood. If I can bring something—some object that belonged to Lyn—she'll be able to tune in to her. That's how she works, by aligning the vibrations from an object with the vibrations of the person who owned it."

"Took me a long time to buy this psychic stuff," said Mike, "but with her, I think you're right. She was spot on about Justina Phillips."

"So that's why I'm here," I said. "What do you have that I can bring to Irene?"

Mike shrugged. "Nothing that I know of. It's like I told you: Lyn was taken away to Chicago by Uncle Frank when she was just a few weeks old." He paused to think, rubbing a slow hand along his jaw. "Naturally, all of her baby clothes went with her, and they took her crib and blankets...the works." He paused again, still thinking. "Wait a minute...we still have Teddy."

"Teddy who?"

"The little stuffed bear that Dad bought for Lyn before she was born. It was always in the crib with her before she was taken to Chicago. Uncle Frank and Aunt Alicia left it behind, so I've kept it all these years since. It's a kind of memento of when Mama and Dad were alive; when we were a family."

"You still have it?"

"Uh...I *think* so. Been a lot of years, but I think I put it in the back bedroom. We use it to store the loose stuff. Wanta have a look?"

"Damn right I do."

We found Teddy, carefully wrapped in white tissue paper, in a neatly-tied cardboard packing box that had been marked "Lyn." Mike said that Carla must have boxed it because he sure didn't.

"No matter how good Hopwood is," Mike said as we were walking back to my Mazda, "how can she tell anything from a toy that a thirty-year-old woman had when she was just a few weeks old?"

"Maybe she won't be able to help," I said. "As I keep saying, we all have psychic abilities to one degree or another. Most of us never learn how to develop it, and even those who do are for the most part only marginally psychic. When someone like Irene Hopwood pops up, with major psychic powers, it's like another Einstein. Far beyond what you or I could ever imagine, let alone attain. So that's what I'm gambling on, Mike. That her powers will help lead me to Lyn."

It was a long speech, but it got my point across.

"Okay, Davey," he said as I got behind the wheel with the

stuffed bear, still in its tissue paper, on the seat beside me. "I just hope this pays off. Keep me in the picture."

"You bet," I said. "Thanks, Mike."

"Hey, the thanks are all mine."

And Teddy and I drove away.

Irene was delighted to see me again. We hadn't been in contact for some time, but she was unchanged. Still regal, still beautifully dressed, her voice still pure velvet. She told me I looked great. Did I work out?

"Less than I know I should," I said. "I get to the gym occassionally...swim in the ocean...hike in the hill country behind my house. I'm trying to develop a regular workout routine. So far, I haven't succeeded. But I *feel* healthy."

Her big Victorian mansion had more antiques in it than I had remembered. There was one particular item I hadn't seen before, a leather-topped rosewood desk she'd placed in the foyer.

"That's new, isn't it?" I asked.

"If you can describe something this old as new, then you're right," she said. "I get a kick out of shopping around for antiques. Found this desk at a shop in Canoga Park.. They've got a whole block of antique shops along Sherman Way. This desk was an incredible bargain. I don't think they knew what they had. When I saw it, I grabbed it."

"A real beauty," I said.

We sat down on a pair of Edwardian high-backed chairs in the library. On a table, already set out, was a plate of chocolate chip cookies and a pot of mint tea. Perfect.

"You know why I'm here," I said, nibbling one of the cookies. (Delicious!) "As I told you on the phone, I've brought an object that once belonged to the subject I'm attempting to trace."

"Male or female?"

"Female. Thirty years old. She had this when she was a very young baby."

I handed Teddy to her.

"You have nothing more recent?"

"No. Her uncle in Chicago probably has stuff of hers that's more recent, but I was hoping you could work with this."

She turned the stuffed toy in her hand. "David, I have to tell you, with something this old..."

"I know. But anything you can pick up from it might provide a lead."

"To where she is right now?"

"Right."

"Sometimes I get vibrations that tell me where the subject has *been*, but that doesn't always mean the person is still at the location I'm envisioning in my mind."

"I understand. But I'm at a total dead end. The trail I followed just petered out."

"I'll do my best," she said. Then: "Please close the drapes. It's difficult to concentrate when there's so much light in the room."

I closed the heavy velvet drapes at each window and returned to my chair. It was now almost dark in the room, which seemed to satisfy Irene.

She was ready to begin.

"So what did she tell you?" Kelly asked me. She was in an emerald-colored pantsuit which matched her eyes. Italian gold earrings sparkled in the reflection of a bright harvest sun. As usual, she looked terrific.

It was early Saturday morning and we were standing in a crowded hall outside Avalon's Casino Ballroom on Catalina Island. Santini's fashion show was due to open its doors any minute and Kelly had already reserved a seat for me inside, two rows back from the runway. As a working journalist, her seat was in the front row.

"I didn't expect much from Irene," I admitted. "Not based on a Teddy bear that hadn't been around its 'owner' for close to thirty years."

"Was she able to read the vibrations?"

"She got some pictures, but they were pretty vague."

"So what did she see?" Kelly was getting impatient.

"An old Western mining town. Weathered buildings. Broken wooden sidewalks. Tumbleweeds blowing down the main street. Everything abandoned."

"A ghost town," said Kelly.

"Yeah," I nodded. "But with no ghosts in it. Just people. Lyn was one of them. At least that was what Irene was getting, this vision of Lyn with other people in this old ghost town. And the people were all alive."

"How long ago?"

"What do you mean?"

"Was it the present, or sometime in the past? How old did Lyn look in the vision?"

"Irene couldn't tell."

"There are hundreds of ghost towns," said Kelly. "Did this one have a name?"

"No—and she wasn't even sure it was in California. Could be in Nevada...Arizona...Montana...almost anywhere."

"Did she envision any words connected with the town? Like painted signs."

"Not at first," I said. "Then she described an old building with wooden pillars at the end of the main street with some faded lettering on the front door. A lot of the paint had flaked away. She could only make out seven letters."

"What were they?"

"She saw part of the word ending in 'NK.' Then, an 'OF,' followed by a 'BOD' with two letters missing."

"The 'NK' could probably mean a bank, since old banks

often had pillars in front—to make them look stable and permanent to jittery customers. The 'OF' is obviously part of 'BANK OF'—but I don't know about the 'BOD' part." Her eyes were looking out at the sea, but her mind was far away, thinking. "Wait! I think I *do* know, but it would be just a guess."

"So guess."

"Several years ago I visited a ghost town with my Dad. It was in northern California, on the other side of Yosemite National Park, down a long dirt road that I think led into Nevada. Bodie. I'm sure it must still be there."

I hugged her. "Kelly girl, you're a bloody marvel! I'll bet that's it. BANK OF BODIE, that's what had to have been painted on the door."

"You can't be sure."

"I'm sure enough to want to check it out myself."

"But what would Lyn Lucero be doing in an abandoned Western ghost town?"

"Maybe looking for ghosts," I said. "Or..." I hesitated, thinking. "There could be another reason. I read something about a mystical cult who claimed they had a direct pipeline to what they called 'The Divine Spirit.' This article said they made their home in 'Bodie, a California ghost town.' Maybe Lyn joined them. It would be just the kind of thing she'd go for."

"Now *you're* guessing," said Kelly.

"What else can I do? If the cult is still there, she could be with them."

"What if they've moved on?"

"I know it's a long shot, but I'm going to Bodie."

"Not until tomorrow, you're not," she said. "We have a *date*, remember?"

I kissed her. "I am completely unable to resist redheads named Kelly. A major weakness of mine."

A buzzer sounded in the hall and the doors opened. The

crowd surged forward, sweeping us into the ballroom. We found our assigned seats in the frenzy as camera crews, still photographers, and other members of the media jockeyed for prime positions next to the runway. Apparently, fashion was big news.

Within minutes the overheads dimmed, the stage curtain parted, and a white spotlight picked out the man himself. Santini, with studied arrogance, began the show by talking about his fashion philosophy, then introduced his premiere line of upscale, "total life" fashion wear.

My mind wasn't on PR performances.

I was thinking of a ghost town named Bodie.

The show lasted two hours. Skinny young models—skinny females and skinny males—paraded along the runway in "evening wear, business wear, leisure wear, and resort wear" (as the program stated). Everything from suitable-for-the-Supreme-Court suits to well-nigh-illegal-in-public Brazilian thongs. Naturally, I liked the thongs better than the attorney wear.

When it was over, Kelly met me outside. We dropped by the hotel to get a bite to eat and change into riding clothes, then took off for a day on the island.

She was a textbook of information about Santa Catalina. She called it "doing my homework," adding that "whenever I go someplace new, I always research it first."

For example, did I know that Santa Catalina was one of approximately twenty Channel Islands, and that these islands were actually visible summits of the now-submerged Sierra Coast range?

I didn't know.

And did I know that Catalina, first sighted by the Portuguese explorer Cabrillo in 1540, is the largest of these islands, at twenty-two miles in length, four miles across at its widest part?

I didn't know that, either.

Kelly's afternoon goal was to find the best possible view of the island, so we rented two horses and proceeded along a trail that climbed the steep side of Descanso Canyon. I'm not much of a rider, and I think my horse knew it. He turned his head and regarded me with what I'm certain was a high degree of contempt. I just ignored him.

But I couldn't ignore the steep climb. Halfway up, rounding a curve where the trail overlooked a sheer drop of a thousand feet to the ocean rocks below, my stomach lurched and I felt a wave of dizziness sweep over me.

"Are you all right?" asked Kelly. "You look kind of green."

"Uh...I'm okay. It's just that I'm allergic to falling a thousand feet off the edge of a canyon." She smiled. "C'mon, you'll love it up top."

"I'm sure I will," I said, urging my horse forward.

At the three-mile summit we dismounted. The panoramic view was indeed spectacular. We could see the entire island, its scattered peaks and ranges extending into ocean mist. Across the water, the mainland and the distant Sierra Madre could be dimly seen to the north.

Then something big skimmed over me and I ducked low, shielding my head. "What the hell was that?"

Kelly was grinning at me. "An American eagle," she said. "They have nests up here."

I watched the giant bird settle along a cliff edge. Probably bringing food to its young. I was glad I wasn't on the menu.

"They also have flying fish here at Catalina," she told me, "but it's a little late in the year for them."

"How big are they?"

"Up to eighteen inches in length," she said. "They have chest fins that function as glider wings to support them in the air. And they're fast."

"*How* fast?"

"They can hit forty miles an hour at takeoff. They use a vibrating tail fin to provide lifting power."

"Okay, now I know everything about flying fish that I care to know," I said.

Kelly laughed and patted my shoulder. "Relax. We're having fun."

"I'll relax once we're back on level ground."

We made it down the canyon without being attacked by wild boars, hungry eagles, or crazed mountain goats, for which I was grateful.

Things got much better that evening when Kelly and I made love on a secluded stretch of palm-fringed beach in an area known as Smuggler's Cove.

Afterward, we lay in the sand, looking up at the stars. Kelly, her head resting on my shoulder, was a warm, loving presence next to me.

"We should get married," she said quietly.

"You're probably right," I said.

"Well, *are* we?"

I shrugged. "How should I know? You have to ask me first."

"No!" she protested. "You're supposed to ask *me*! That's how it goes."

"You need to remind me to ask," I said.

"When should I remind you?"

"In about six months, I think. I should be ready by then."

"You're impossible," said Kelly. She kissed me.

And we made love again.

*   *   *

September, 1998

He was a stubborn, practical man who had spent the greater part of his boyhood in Missouri, the "Show Me" state. The motto suited him just fine—because he scoffed at anything supernatural or paranormal. Only weak-brained people believed in such things. It was all balderdash, a word his mother had used for anything that was ridiculous.

"Those goings-on in Washington," she'd say to him. "Balderdash. Every bit of it."

He watched a lot of football on TV, but he didn't have a favorite team. He liked them all. He'd played running back for his high school team the Jefferson Jets. He was big and tough and aggressive, so he'd done very well at football. Had he gone on to college, he might have become a grid-iron star, but his working-class parents couldn't afford to send him, so he stayed in Jefferson and sold automobile tires for Firestone.

Then his aunt died and he inherited ten thousand dollars. In his day (he was now in his sixties), that was a pile of money. You could do a lot with ten thousand dollars.

By then he was tired of living in the Midwest, with its humid summers and icebound winters, so he quit his job and took a train out to California. He wasn't afraid of earthquakes, and he'd never have to deal with frozen pipes again.

He settled in Los Angeles and became a tree trimmer for the city. He enjoyed being outdoors in the always-mild weather—except for July and August when it got too hot for his taste. Not the kind of humid Midwest heat he'd grown up with, but a dry, desert heat that was almost as bad. Going into his second summer he quit trimming trees and moved to San Jose, where it was cooler in the summer, and where a first cousin of his owned a downtown store: Charlie's Hardware

He hired on as a clerk and soon worked his way up to manager. Then he met a waitress with dyed hair who was divorced. She had two boys, aged five and six. She came on to him strong, the way those cheerleaders back in Jefferson used to come on to him when he scored touchdowns. Not long after, he scored a touchdown with the waitress. They got married. He liked the idea of a ready-made family and thought he'd make a good father. He told the boys to call him "Pop."

The marriage went sour when she got hooked on drugs. First, the county took her kids away and put them into foster care. She didn't seem to mind. All she wanted was drugs, so he left her and filed for divorce. He didn't intend to stay married to a druggie.

His cousin Charlie got into financial trouble playing the commodities market and had to shut down the hardware store. That was just a month after his divorce became final. His cousin said the big chain stores had stolen all his customers, but that wasn't true. It was the commodities market that did him in.

That's when the night watchman quit at Winchester House and he got offered the job. Why had the other guy quit? Because he said that weird things had been going on inside the house at night; the watchman got real nervous about being there, so he walked.

The property manager asked him a lot of fool questions.

Did he believe in spirits of the dead?

No.

Did he believe in demonic possession?

No.

Did he believe that Winchester House was haunted?

Hell, no!

People were said to have disappeared inside Winchester House, including a gardener who tended the grounds. A tourist had died in there for sure, which was why it had been closed to the public. The death was never explained. Did any of this bother him?

Not at all. If they were looking for a reliable night watchman, they didn't have to look any further. He was their man. He'd never been afraid of anything in his life, and he could guarantee they'd be happy they hired him.

Fine. He had the job.

Were there any other guards at Winchester House? Yes, he was told, but only on the day and early evening shifts. He'd be the only one there at night. Great. That meant he could be his own boss and wouldn't have to take orders from a senior watchman. That was correct, they said. After the first week of training, once he'd learned the routine, he'd be strictly on his own.

Okay, then. He was ready for Winchester House.

On his first night alone nothing happened.

One his second night, nothing happened.

However, on his third night...

He was making his rounds, enjoying the solitude with the hushed night darkness cloaking him. He'd walked around to the north side of the house when he glanced up at a third-story window and saw the figure.

A woman, standing motionless there, staring down at him.

Damn! The house was suppose to be empty. No one was allowed inside, so what was this woman doing at an upstairs window? She had no business in there, no legal right to be in the building.

He'd go in, find her, and turn her over to the San Jose police as a trespasser.

He hadn't been able to make out any features in the dimness of the upper room. And she hadn't moved, just stood there, staring down at him.

A ghost? He chuckled to himself. That's the one thing he was certain of—the woman was real. Not misty or transparent. Three-dimensional. Real. He knew what he'd seen.

"All right, lady," he murmured. "Time to move your ass outta there."

Fumbling in his jacket for the emergency house keys, he walked to the side entrance closest to the upper window. The ring of keys jingled faintly in his hand as he selected one. Inserted it. Didn't fit. Nor did the next two. But the fourth one turned easily in the lock and the door clicked open.

He didn't carry a gun. Wasn't authorized. But he was licensed to carry a canister of Mace, and if she gave him any trouble he wouldn't hesitate to use it. Some women are strong, and can be dangerous. He'd take no chances with her.

He'd only been in the house twice, both during the day, so he could get the general bearings of the property. Now, in the darkness, with the strong white beam of his tri-cell flashlight revealing a veritable maze of rooms, stairs, and hallways, he hesitated. He must be careful or he could get lost in the warren of passageways.

The room where he'd seen the woman should be almost directly above him. A polished wooden stairway, with black rubber matting fitted to each step, led upward. He began the climb, stepping lightly. No use warning her he was coming. Better to surprise her if at all possible.

The stairs veered left, but after making the turn he was astonished to see them dead end at a solid wall. The staircase led nowhere.

Served him right. He'd been warned about such things. The place was said to be filled with false doors, fake closets, drawers that were never meant to open, and dead-end stairways. He should have used the elevator which was on this side of the house. Fine, he'd do that, even if the noise warned the intruder.

He retraced his steps, guided by the flash beam, and moved down the lower hall to the ancient wrought iron elevator. He pressed a small ivory button set into the wall and the cage door opened with a dry, rasping sound.

He entered the small, cramped cage—designed to hold the little old lady who built the place and no one else—and pressed an inside button marked "3." The elevator creaked into motion, grinding its way slowly upward. Well, the intruder would know he was coming now, but that was okay. He'd find her. He was sure of himself. And not at all nervous. Nothing to be nervous about. Just do the job he'd been hired for.

That was when the elevator stopped.

He was suddenly angry. First the vanishing stairs and now some malfunction in this stupid Victorian relic. He rattled the cage door. It wouldn't budge. He stabbed the three buttons on the cage wall. Nothing. What to do? Shouting for help would be a waste of time because the only other person in the building was the woman he'd come in to arrest. Would you mind helping me, lady, so I can turn you over to the cops? He was trying to think of a way out when he noticed something at his feet.

A thick, dark liquid was seeping across the floor of the cage. It smelled of copper. Was there a leak somewhere? What was this stuff? Then...he knew. Incredible, but he knew.

It was blood.

Abruptly, the elevator jolted into life, resuming its slow upward grind. He was still staring down at the spreading pool of blood when the cage stopped and the door folded back. He arrived on the third floor.

I won't think about the damn blood, he told himself, or why it was there, or where it came from. No, I'll just think of the woman I have to catch. Just do my job.

He faced a long, dark hallway. She'd been standing at the window of a room halfway down, by his reckoning. Was she still in there? Probably not, but that was the place to start. He beamed his flash ahead of him and followed the path of light.

Then he snapped off his flash. A thin line of dim yellow outlined a door in the middle of the hall. A lamp was on in that room!

He walked cautiously to the door, listening for inside movement. Only silence.

All right, lady, if you're there, I'm coming in to get you.

He pulled out his canister of Mace, flipped off the safety, and gripped it firmly.

Then he turned the handle of the door. It swung open.

Something rushed at him. Something monstrous. He was hit, spun around, his back to the third-floor window. He released the Mace at a mass that struck him with violent force, but there was no reaction from this creature.

He fell. Backward. Through the window, the glass sharding around his body in bright pieces. Down. Directly into...

The spear-tipped iron fence which separated the lawn from the garden.

Impaled on the fence, his blood running thick and coppery into the grass, he could still see her.

Standing at the window, motionless, staring down at him.

*   *   *

Bodie is just where Kelly said it was, north of Yosemite, not far from the Nevada border.

I rented a Jeep for my trip. You need a vehicle with high road clearance and 4-wheel drive for a trip like this.

I took the Antelope Valley route almost to Victorville, then turned left on Highway 395 for the long run north. I would be going past Yosemite, then would turn east before I got to Bridgeport. It was a full day's trip on secondary highways up most of the state. I stopped at the "halfway" point in Bishop to eat and gas up, then settled in for a long afternoon on the road.

The highway to Bodie, legally designated as 270, was clearly marked as I made the easy right turn east. Soon I drove by a caution sign:

> BODIE GHOST TOWN
> 13 MILES
> WARNING!
> ROUGH ROAD
> CLOSED IN WINTER

A crudely-painted arrow pointed toward a stretch of unpaved dirt leading into the hills.

The sign was right. The road was indeed rough, pitted with deep ruts and potholes. I was jolted and shaken as I followed the winding road into a range of stark brown hills. On a couple of occasions, when I hit sunken boulders, I tensed my stomach muscles, but the Jeep forged onward like a faithful horse. I had visions of a helicopter circling the route, photographing my progress. It would have been a perfect TV Jeep commercial.

Finally, as I reached the brow of a slight grade, there it was, spread below me.

Bodie.

Inspired by Kelly's example, I'd searched the Internet for information before I left L.A. In the 1880s, Bodie was one of the West's most notorious mining towns, with no less than sixty-five saloons, plus dozens of cribs and elegant bagnios which enlisted the talents of such colorful ladies of the night as Madame Moustache, Rosa Mae of Maiden Lane, Nine-finger Annie, and Aurora O'Reilly, the Irish Hellcat. In fact, the preacher who tended his flock at Bodie's Methodist Church had called the town "a sea of sin, fired by rotgut whiskey, and lashed by the tempests of untrammeled lust."

There was no lust in evidence, untrammeled or otherwise, as I scanned the raw, paint-scoured wooden buildings below me, brown as cured leather. A cold October wind moaned between the barren hills which surrounded the town, raising frisky dust devils in the dirt street. The wind whined through corrugated iron sidings, whipped the tawny high grass and sagebrush, and sent big tumbleweeds rolling along the warped, sun-blasted boardwalks.

Hell of a place to live, I thought, moving down a graveled incline from the parking area into the heart of Bodie. If a cult actually flourished here, I saw no evidence of it. Maybe they'd come and gone, or maybe they'd never been here at all.

The whole place depressed me, and I had no sense of Lyn Lucero. Yet I found the pillared bank building at the end of Main Street, and the flake-painted letters were visible on the door:

NK OF BOD

Proof of Irene Hopwood's psychic powers. Obviously, I was wrong about Lyn. Irene's vision confirmed the fact that she had been here. I decided to explore the town to see if I could turn up any cult members who might know something about her.

I passed the two-story school with a tattered letter from a local youngster pasted in the window ("We love Bodie!"), then walked into one of the saloons. It had a faro table in one corner and a row of rusted slot machines lined up along the wall like rusted iron soldiers.

The town jail had triple-bunk cells, with the cell doors

standing open. An ancient, wood-burning stove squatted in the center of the jail office, and there was a reward poster, edges curling, tacked to the wall:

WANTED!

WASHOE PETE AKA

ROUGH-AND-TUMBLE JACK

THE BAD MAN OF BODIE

FIVE HUNDRED DOLLAR REWARD,

DEAD OR ALIVE

I wondered if they'd ever caught up with old Pete; he sounded like bad medicine. There was a photo of a man named Big Knuckle Thompson in an oval wood frame next to the poster. I leaned forward to read the brass plaque beneath it:

SHERIFF OF BODIE, 1860-1865.

KILLED IN THE LINE OF DUTY.

Maybe Washoe Pete had done him in.

I left the jail and walked past the firehouse and stables. An old iron wagon, with missing wheels, was parked in front of the blacksmith's, and an anvil, with some long-handled tongs used for hot horseshoes, was inside.

I walked into the office of the town's newspaper, *The Bodie Daily Press.* A flake-yellowed front page was mounted behind cracked glass next to a time-ruptured printing press. I rubbed the heel of my hand across the dust-grimed surface to read:

BODIE NOW QUIET

LULL IN DAILY KILLINGS

The story beneath the headline reported that "Bodie may be on the way to respectability, since no one has been shot or stabbed here during the last seven days."

I proceeded along Main once more to the Odd Fellows Hall, and was startled to see a man seated near one of the windows fronting the street.

I went inside and he turned in my direction. He had a long, untrimmed beard, a mat of wildly-tossed hair, and narrow, slate-colored eyes. His clothes were ragged but clean.

"Been watchin' you walkin' back and forth out there," he said. "Pretty cold this time'a year for tourists."

"I'm no tourist," I said. "I'm here for a reason."

"That bein'?"

"I'm looking for a woman. She might have joined a cult based here in Bodie."

"Wish they'd quit callin' us that. What we are is a family. Not blood-related, but just as close-knit."

"And you're a member?"

He nodded. "Right proud to say I belong to the Grand Pentacles of the Divine Spirit."

"Can't say I've heard of them."

"They live on Mars. Underground city. Got a big, fat-ass spaceship they come to Earth in ever few years to pick up folks that wanta go live on Mars."

"How come you're not living there?"

"We rep 'em here on Earth. The Pentacles hafta have human representatives to let folks know about 'em. We recruit people, like the Army an' Navy."

"I see. How many of you are there...in the family?"

"Mebbe a dozen of us left. At one time, two, three years ago, we had as many as fifty-plus folks livin' here."

"Are the others on Mars?" I asked with a straight face.

"Nope. Some took off the first winter. More the next. Each year, when the bad weather kicks in, we lose folks. An' it's gonna be another pisser this year. Got us some heavy snow comin' up swift. You kin feel it in the wind. Winters are hard to take in Bodie."

"I'm sure they are." I smiled at him. "Have you ever heard of a woman name Lyn Lucero? About thirty. Dark haired. Very attractive."

His answer surprised me.

"Sure. We called her Linnie. Real sweet she was. Come here seekin' the Divine Spirit. Only with us for a couple months, though. Then she told us we were fulla crap and left."

"When was that?"

"Bout this time last year. Late October. Took off real sudden one day. Said she'd had enough lies fed to her, so she just took off."

"When she first came here...she believed that you people were actually in contact with a Divine Spirit?"

"Not 'a' Spirit! *The* Spirit! And we *are*. We got us a direct Earth-to-Mars connection."

I nodded. "Where are your other members?"

"In the old buildings on the hill. They live up there at the mine. Me, too, but today I thought I'd come into town an' watch the tumbleweeds go by. Wind really whips 'em along."

"Yes, it does." I cleared my throat, tried another smile. "Would you happen to know when Lyn...uh, Linnie...where she went after she left here?"

I didn't expect him to know, but he surprised me again.

"Sure," he said. "I know where she went. She told us where."

"What did she tell you?"

"She'd been readin; about this spook place in San Jose. Called Winchester House. Figured she could maybe hook up with a ghost or two at that place. So that's where she went—to Winchester House."

"Thanks for the information," I said. "Really appreciate all your help."

"You bet. Good luck in findin' Linnie. If you do, be sure an' tell her hello from Old Tom." He chuckled. "That's what they call me, Old Tom, even though I just hit forty. Middle-aged Tom would be more to the truth of it, wouldn't you say?"

"Maybe it's the beard," I told him. "It can age a man."

"Could be. Well, don't forget my hello," he said as I walked out of the Odd Fellows Hall.

"I won't forget," I said.

Five minutes later I was fighting the pitted road to 395, hoping there was an open restaurant and a vacant motel room waiting for me in Bridgeport.

San Jose, called the "Garden City," famed for its prunes, grapes, plums, peaches, and apricots, is located in the fertile Santa Clara Valley south of San Francisco. Winchester House is just a few minutes away from the downtown area on Winchester Boulevard, between Stevens Creek and I-280.

I was convinced that this trip was leading to another dead end in my search. Sure, I was all but certain that Lyn had been to Winchester House, seeking to "hook up with a ghost or two" (as Old Tom had put it), but that was approximately a year ago. Where she went after leaving San Jose was the key question, and there was no one to ask.

My first stop in town was Nico's Greek restaurant where I had a huge platter or orektika, mixed appetizers, followed by the honeyed decadence of a shredded-wheat-and-chopped-nut first cousin to baklava. After that, with my stomach at peace, I decided to check out the San Jose Police Department in the extremely vague hope that they might have some information on Lyn.

Maybe she had done something to attract their attention. Maybe she'd assaulted a cop and was cooling her heels in the local jail. And maybe I'll grow wings and fly to Mars so I can join the Grand Pentacles of the Divine Spirit. Ah, well. In an investigation, you go with what you've got.

"What's the problem?" the desk sergeant asked me. He had horse teeth and a very large nose.

"I guess I need to see someone in Missing Persons," I said. The tentative tone of my voice betrayed my uncertainty.

"You *guess*? Meaning you don't know who you want to see?"

"I'm looking for a woman who visited Winchester House within the past twelve months," I told him.

"You know how many lady tourists visit there each year?" he asked.

"No, and please don't tell me," I said. "Just send me to someone I can talk to about this woman."

"Waste of time, if you ask me."

"Look, all I want to do is talk to somebody about—"

"Okay, okay," he cut in. "Lemme buzz Lieutenant Willard. Maybe he'll talk to you."

Five minutes later Willard showed up and gestured for me to follow him back to his office. He was a beefcake in a starched white shirt that showed off his muscles. A dark blue cast to his skin told me he needed to shave twice a day. When he spoke, I wondered about steroids; his voice reminded me of a bullfrog.

We sat down in his office, which was a shade less cluttered than Mike's. He leaned back in a creaking swivel chair and regarded me with the standard cop's stare.

"How can I help you, Mister..."

"Kincaid. David Kincaid."

"What is it you do?"

"I work in the field of the paranormal," I said.

"Spook city, eh?" He grinned. He either led a very healthy life or he'd paid a fortune so his dentist could create perfect teeth. I was impressed.

"Right now I'm trying to locate the sister of a homicide cop, friend of mine in Malibu."

"I used to surf off Malibu," Willard said. "Caught some nice ones you could ride all the way in to the beach. Yeah, I was really a board freak in those days. Till I moved up here. Water up here's too cold to surf. Now I just look at pictures."

"His sister's name is Lyn Lucero," I said, trying to get the conversation back in focus.

"Describe her."

"Dark-haired. About thirty. Good figure. Very attractive."

"Got a photo?"

"No."

Willard grunted, shifting in his chair.

"What with Stanford, and the lure of Frisco, and the money in Silicon Valley, we got missing foxes out the ass," he said. "I'm not gonna be able to help you, Kincaid."

"Actually, I didn't expect you'd have anything on her," I admitted. "All I know is she came here to visit Winchester House."

"Like a zillion others," he said. "Place is famous around the world. Jerry Godfrey, editor at the San Jose *Mercury*, told me that last year, when he was in Mongolia, out in the countryside somewhere, he discovered a bumper sticker on the wall: I VISITED THE WINCHESTER MYSTERY HOUSE. You see the problem?"

"Yeah," I said. "Thousands of tourists every year, and none of them memorable enough to stand out." I hesitated. "What hours is it open?"

"It's not. We closed it last November when a tourist died there under mysterious circumstances."

"The tourist was murdered?"

"Well, his head was ripped off, so I guess you can rule out suicide."

"And they *closed* it? Doesn't closing Winchester House impact the local economy?"

"Sure does. But not long after the tourist was murdered, a gardener disappeared—and just a month ago we found the night watchman impaled on a fence. He fell out of a three-story window. Nobody knows what he was doing on the third floor. Then...there's other stuff."

"What other stuff?"

"The tower bell ringing at midnight...pipe organ playing in the ballroom...funny lights in some of the windows...crazy stuff like that. Probably some local high school kids playing ghost."

"Have you had the house searched?"

"We've done our best. Trouble is, there's a hundred and sixty rooms in that place, and a lot of them are blocked off. Add in the secret passages and hidden doors and it'd take a whole damn army to do a thorough job. And we don't have an army."

"I see your problem."

"The old gal who used to live there never installed any burglar alarms, so that makes things even tougher. The management is too cheap to hire more than one night watchman, and one's not enough—not for a place like that."

"I'd like to know more about the place," I said. "History...background...a full description."

"Hold on a sec," said Willard.

He got up and walked to a dented gray filing cabinet next to the door. He opened the top drawer and thumbed through some folders, then handed me a thick paperback.

The title: *A Reference Guide To The Winchester Mystery House.*

"That's pretty complete," Willard said. "You can keep it. I got plenty more."

"Thanks for your time," I said.

"Hey..." He shrugged. "It's what I get paid for."

I was in no hurry to enter Winchester House. In fact, since the place was closed, I knew I'd have to break in at night. At least I didn't have any burglar alarms to worry about. All I had to do was avoid being seen by the watchman.

Why did I want to go inside the house, ignoring the law and risking arrest for trespassing, when I knew damn well that Lyn Lucero had long since come and gone? A perplexing question, and one I didn't have any real answer for. It was just that somehow I had to do this. I was possessed of an overwhelming sense of the necessity to go in there. Could be my psychic power manifesting itself. Certainly it was far more than curiosity; it was a *compulsion*.

But, as I've stated, I was in no hurry, knowing I had to wait for darkness. Which left me the rest of the day to learn about what made Winchester House so famous.

The book I'd obtained at police headquarters was chock full of startling facts about the house and the bizarre woman who had built it.

Born in 1840, Sarah Pardee had married the man who manufactured the Winchester rifle, William Wirt Winchester, in 1862. They lost their infant daughter to a "mysterious illness" in 1866, and within fifteen years, Winchester himself was dead.

Sarah believed that she was cursed by the tortured spirits of those who had been killed by bullets from a Winchester. She consulted a medium in Boston who verified her fears, and ordered her to move West and build, for the spirits, a great house "made of the most costly woods, crystals, and metals." She must constantly add to this house, and so long as construction continued, she would be safe from all supernatural forces.

"You alone," the medium had told her, "can appease the

spirits of those countless victims of the Winchester rifle."

Sarah did exactly as ordered, moving to California's Santa Clara Valley in 1884, where she purchased a small eight-room farmhouse on a dirt road three miles west of San Jose. Immediately, she hired several carpenters to begin expanding the house. Working them in shifts around the clock, Sarah made sure that the construction continued every hour of every day throughout the year. The sawing, sanding, and hammering at Winchester House never ceased, day or night for the next thirty-eight years until her death in 1922.

The results of all this are truly *amazing*.

Covering six full acres, the house contains one hundred and sixty rooms, forty-seven stairways, two thousand doors, ten thousand windows, forty bedrooms, six kitchens, three elevators, forty-seven fireplaces, and miles of twisting hallways. There's a servant's wing, a bell tower, stables, a hayloft, four fountains, a plumber's shop, an aviary, a gas plant, a 3-story water-tower, and a plush ballroom large enough for a hundred dancing couples.

During Sarah Winchester's tenure at the house, freight trains rolled into San Jose loaded with gold-and-silver chandeliers, Persian silks, Tiffany leaded glass, bronze-inlaid doors, uncounted rolls of imported Lincrusta wallpaper, and over a hundred varieties of tree and plant life from around the globe. The floors were of rare hardwoods, and many walls were inset with teak, white ash, and rosewood.

Each night Sarah would wend her way through the vast house and enter her Blue Room where she would dim the gaslights and confer with her "friendly thirteen." These were the thirteen spirits who sided with her against others who would do her harm. To confuse her "enemy spirits," Sarah added secret passageways, blind chimneys, hidden trapdoors, stairs that dead-ended in ceilings and blank walls, fake closets, and doors that opened into space.

Sarah would sleep in a different bedroom each night in order to further baffle her enemy shades.

The book mentioned that some tourists had complained about blood seeping from an oil painting of a wounded Indian, doorknobs turning in empty corridors, and frightening images appearing in bathroom mirrors. One elderly woman was terrified when the lid on a small music box popped open in one of the bedrooms and a black snake slithered out, to disappear through a crack in the floor.

A giant bird with coal-red eyes was seen in one hallway. Voices were heard in empty rooms, and open windows suddenly slammed shut.

One of the most bizarre aspects of Sarah Winchester was her fixation on the number 13. The book listed:

> 13 BATHROOMS
> 13 PANES IN THE STAINED-GLASS WINDOWS
> 13 RAILS BENEATH A SKYLIGHT
> 13 CUPOLAS IN THE GREENHOUSE
> 13 FAN PALMS ALONG THE FRONT DRIVE
> 13 CEILING PANELS IN A BEDROOM
> 13 GAS JETS IN THE BALLROOM CHANDELIER
> 13 DRAIN HOLES IN THE KITCHEN SINKS
> 13 HOOKS IN THE BLUE ROOM TO HOLD HER
> "SPIRIT ROBES"

And Sarah's will consisted of 13 parts, which she signed 13 times.

All this, I thought, to placate her thirteen friendly spirits.

Was Sarah Pardee Winchester insane—or were there paranormal forces active in Winchester House that defied science and logic?

By midnight, I would have my answer.

Halloween Night

The holiday surprised me. I'd been so absorbed in the Lucero case that I hadn't realized that I would be entering Winchester House on Halloween. But enter it I would.

I was concerned with the possibility of increased security at the house on this particular night. To keep away locals who might figure this was the perfect time to pull some Halloween hijinks inside the place.

But when I arrrived at the site, shortly after full darkness had set in, I was relieved to find just the single night guard on duty. Sure, he'd be on special alert for the holiday, but I was certain of my ability to penetrate the house without being detected.

I crouched in the thick bushes, watching him make his rounds as he checked all of the outside doors and flashed his light through windows and between trees. He walked leisurely, humming softly to himself, a pale, pudgy, thick-browed fellow smoking a briar pipe. Little blue puffs of tobacco smoke accompanied him as he walked.

When he completed his rounds near the front of the house, and moved toward the water tower in the rear, I glided quickly over to a side door and inserted a thin sliver of steel into the keyhole. Mike had taught me the art of opening doors this way, and now his instructions paid off. I felt the lock give, and the knob turned easily under my hand.

Inside, I used the same technique to relock the door, then removed a small metal flashlight from my jacket. I had taped the clear end in order to narrow the beam. Didn't want to attract the guard's attention. And I made sure to stay clear of the windows which fronted the grounds. If he saw moving lights inside, he'd certainly investigate that.

What did I expect to find now what I was finally inside Winchester House? I didn't know. An irresistible compulsion had drawn me here, but I had no idea why.

I walked down a short length of corridor and entered one of the interior bedrooms, swinging the beam of my flash around the large chamber. Impressive. The floor was polished rosewood, and two velvet-backed chairs flanked a small marble table near two heavily-draped windows. The bed had a high, intricately carved headboard, and the pillows were trimmed in white lace.

I moved to the large mirror above the dressing table and felt the hair rise along the back of my neck. Behind my reflection, something was moving in the corner of the room.

Spinning around, I centered my light beam on the object.

A woman's shoe, of the high-button type worn in Victorian times. It was sliding along the polished floor toward me.

I stared at it.

The shoe suddenly leaped upward, striking me hard to the chest. With stunning force, as if someone strong had kicked me. I staggered back under the blow as the shoe dropped to the floor.

Now it was motionless.

I left the bedroom thinking: Kincaid, you've just been attacked by a lady's shoe. In my paranormal career, this was definitely a first. Okay then, what was next? So far as I was concerned, Winchester House was living up to its reputation. Spectral forces indeed existed here.

Back in the corridor I got another shock. A message had been scrawled in large red letters (blood?) on the white embossed wallpaper next to the bedroom door:

LEAVE THIS HOUSE
YOU ARE NOT WELCOME HERE

The message didn't seem real. It read like a Halloween joke—or a warning from one of Mike's old *Wu Fang* pulps. Yet, there it was. And no doubt meant just for me. I'd passed that area of wall in entering the bedroom and it had been clear. Someone had written the message while I was inside the room.

Should I heed the warning and leave? I was sorely tempted to get the hell out of the place, but if I left now I'd never find out *why* I'd been compelled to come here. After all, I was a professional paranormal investigator; I'd encountered such phenomena in the past. I should feel challenged, not frightened.

Yet somehow this situation was different. I felt oppressive danger here that I had never previously experienced.

I kept telling myself: Kincaid, you're here for a reason. Solve the mystery. Learn the reason.

So I stayed.

A fold-out map of Winchester House had been bound into the book Willard had given me and I had studied it carefully. The house interior was far too complex for me to absorb in full detail, but I *did* want to see the Grand Ballroom and, eventually, the Blue Room, and I'd memorized these sections of the map. I should be able to find my way without getting lost. At least, I hoped so.

I was nearing the middle of a long, central hallway when I saw the creature. A huge bird, twice the size of a man, with a hooked razor beak and fiery red eyes, was flapping toward me, its wings beating at the walls to either side. A giant eagle? No, I'd never seen a bird like this one.

The thing was almost on top of me before I managed to duck into a side parlor, jamming the slide-door shut. I could hear the creature's beaked head chopping at the inlaid wood panels. They were almost cracking; at this rate, the bird would slash its way through in bare minutes. I knew I had to find another way out.

Back of the room. Window overlooking a hallway. Locked. I tried to get it open, but couldn't. Used my elbow to try to smash the glass. No luck. Then I spotted an iron poker beside the fireplace. Perfect. I could easily shatter the glass with it.

But the chopping sounds had ceased. Silence. Snapping off my flash, I edged toward the door in the thick darkness, the iron poker in my hand. Slowly, I pulled the door wide.

Nothing!

I beamed the flash along the hallway. Silent and empty.

The creature had vanished.

I shone my beam on the outside of the door. The wood paneling was unmarked.

How could this be? That bird-thing was real. Solid and menacing. Or *was* it? Had I conjured it up from my own vivid imagination? No, not possible. I touched the sore spot on my chest; it was swollen. The shoe was real and so was the bird. I'd seen it as clearly as the furniture in this room.

Then why had it vanished?

I needed to find some answers.

Which is when I heard the music. Heavy and sonorous. It pulsed through the house, the ponderous notes vibrating in my ears. Again, not my imagination.

Someone was playing the pipe organ in the Grand Ballroom.

I slipped the map from my jacket and ran the lightbeam over it. From my point of entry, plus the location of the parlor, I traced the way to the ballroom.

A stairway leading up, then down. A short hallway. Through one of the kitchens. A longer hallway. Then...I was there.

I stood outside the sliding brass doors that separated me from the Grand Ballroom. The sonorous music continued, booming around me with a sentient life of its own.

Surely this must have alerted the night guard. He might arrive here at any second. No matter. I had to confront whoever or whatever was playing the organ.

I pushed open the sliding doors, stepping into...silence. The room was dark and totally deserted. I aimed my flash at the organ. No one sat at the keys of the tall, many-piped instrument, and not a whisper of sound issued from it.

My pulse was racing. I'd never encountered anything like this, not personally. I'd heard stories of pianos and horns that played themselves in the night, of radio and television sets that turned on and off without being touched—but the stark reality I faced here in Winchester House was something I was unprepared for.

I felt caught up in a waking nightmare, with no rational explanation for what was happening.

The guard didn't show. Could it be that he was not meant to hear the sounds I had heard? Was the house putting on a special show, just for me?

I flashed my light around the room. At the hanging chandelier, at the ornate fireplace, at the expensive fitted parquet flooring, its rare woods put together with wooden pegs. Then I left, closing the doors behind me.

The Blue Room. The chamber where Sarah Winchester conducted her nightly séances. That's where I knew I must go. That's where all of my questions would be answered.

Rechecking the map in order to find my way, I started down another long corridor, my flash beam probing the dark. It seemed almost tangible, this thick blackness, as if I might reach out and part it like a curtain.

Suddenly...*cold*. I was moving through intense, freezing cold. Further proof of active paranormal activity. The cold ended when I turned down another sharply-angled hallway.

The passage was becoming narrower. My beam revealed that the walls to either side were swelling like diseased flesh, actually expanding. Realizing that I'd be crushed between them unless I took quick action, I ducked into a kitchen area and paused to lean against a white enamel sink to calm my thudding heart.

Abruptly, with a hissing sound, a long-bladed kitchen knife whipped toward me from the other side of the room. I dived to the linoleum floor as the wicked blade buried itself in a wooden drawer two inches above my head!

I sucked in breath and scrambled to my feet. Out to an adjoining hallway. Up a flight of stairs. Into another corridor. The door just ahead flew off its hinges and spun toward me. I dived sideways into...a library. I was on my hands and knees just beneath a tall, glass-paneled bookcase. The bookcase abruptly tipped downward. I rolled free of its path as it smashed to the floor next to me in a splintering of wood and glass, books cascading from its shelves.

I stood up, shaking, dry-mouthed, breath rattling in my throat. Instinct shouted within me: Get out! *Now! Get out of this hellish place any way you can!*

No, dammit. No! I'd find the Blue Room and confront whatever horror awaited me there. I was compelled to go forward, just as I had been *compelled* to come to this house.

Corridors. Hallways. Stairs. Running blindly. Somehow I would end up where I was destined to be.

The Blue Room.

I was standing just outside it. Breathing hard, my heart pounding, I eased open the door.

The room lived up to its name: it was bathed in a spectral blue light. I saw the table with occult symbols carved into its wood surface, where Sarah would sit alone each night. The chair she sat in. The thirteen hooks on the wall for her spirit robes.

And I saw Lyn Lucero.

No mistake, the figure that stood at the far end of the room was Lyn. Beautiful, and it was obvious from the family resemblance that she was Mike's sister.

She started at me, her eyes reflecting the strange blue

light in the room.

"I've been searching for you, Lyn," I said. "Thought I'd never find you."

"Lyn is dead," said the standing figure. Its voice was deep and rasping. "We control her. We live within her corpse."

The skin of my face felt taut, like stretched fabric. I found it almost impossible to speak—but I knew that this meeting had been pre-determined and that I must find my final answers here. Now.

"Who are you?" I asked.

"We are the Thirteen," the Lyn-thing said. "Sarah Winchester summoned us to destroy those who would invade her house."

"And...when Lyn came here...you *took* her...possessed her flesh?"

"Yes. Her body is our vessel. It serves us."

"What about me?"

"You will die, here in this room," said the Lyn-thing. "Your head will be torn from your neck, your heart will be ripped from your chest—and your blood will flow into the blood of Winchester House."

The thing glided across the floor, toward me. Its legs did not move, yet its body was coming at me in a horrific swooping glide. Its eyes burned with blue fire.

I snatched up the chair and flung it at the advancing corpse. The thing raised a hand—and the chair disintegrated in mid-air.

"We control the elements of Winchester House," the rasping voice informed me. "There is no way you can harm us. Now...we shall have your head."

Backed to the wall, I felt the steel grip of the thing's clawing fingers close around my throat. They began to twist...

"No! Let him go!"

The words boomed through the room.

The Lyn-thing's hands dropped away from my neck and its face—Lyn's face—looked suddenly agonized.

A pale mist in the doorway had materialized into the form of an old woman. Hair in a tight bun. Victorian dress. High-button shoes.

The ghost of Sarah Winchester.

"There has been enough killing," she declared. "I want no more blood spilled in this house. Leave her! I command that you leave her!"

The Lyn-thing quivered and convulsed, writhing, slowly settling to the floor. A final convulsion rippled through it. Then it was motionless.

I drew a long, shuddering breath.

Turned to thank Sarah Winchester.

She was gone.

The doorway was empty.

Lyn Lucero's lifeless body lay face down on the blue floor.

According to the family's wishes, Lyn's body was cremated. Carla, the two girls, Mike's Uncle Frank and Aunt Alicia, and I stood beside him on the beach at Malibu as he scattered her ashes into the incoming surf, letting the tide carry them out to sea.

"I'm sorry, Mike. I didn't want it to end this way."

"We all end this way," Mike said. "We all die." He hesitated and tears glittered along his cheeks. "At least she's at peace now. That's what matters."

We all stood there, watching the tide roll in...roll out...as it has done since the Earth was new.

About the Author

Best known as the author of *Logan's Run* (global bestseller, MGM movie, CBS television series, and—in the near future—a mega-film release from Warner Bros.), William F. Nolan has 90 books, 40 film/TV scripts, and over 700 magazine sales to his credit. His work has been selected for more than 330 anthologies and textbooks, and he is also a poet, artist, and playwright.

Among many honors, Nolan won the "Silver Medal for Excellence" from the Independent Publishers of America, and is twice winner of the Edgar Allen Poe Special Award. He was cited by the American Library Association, has won two Golden Medallions in Europe, and (in 2002) was voted an official "Living Legend in Horror/Dark Fantasy" by the International Horror Guild. He was also voted "Author Emeritus for 2006" by the Science Fiction Writers of America, and won the Stoker "Life Achievement Award" from the Horror Writers of America in 2010.

Nolan lives in Vancouver, WA with 4,000 of his favorite books and a stuffed gorilla.

CPSIA information can be obtained at www.ICGtesting.com
Printed in the USA
BVOW08s1413210714

359935BV00028B/429/P